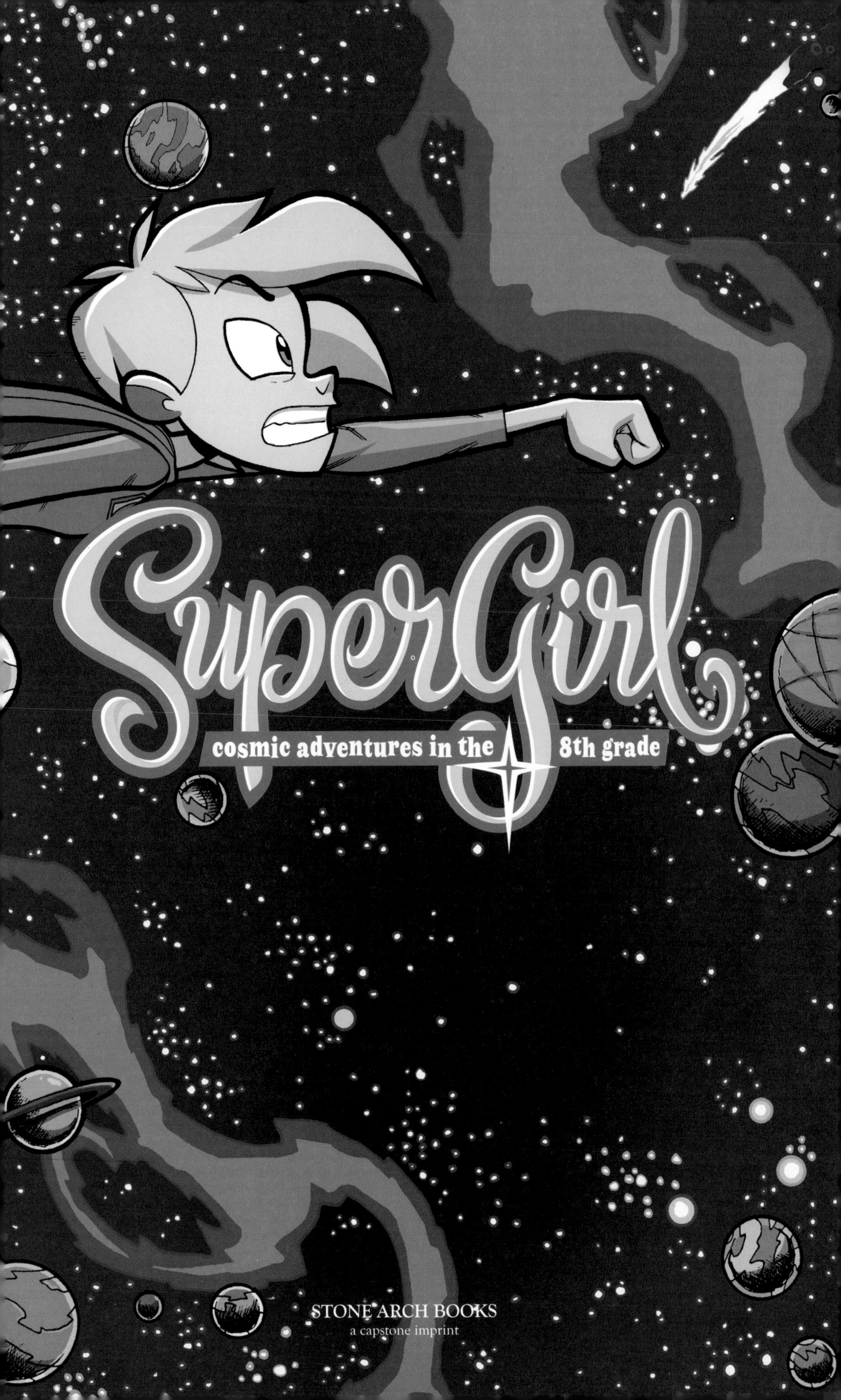
SuperGirl
cosmic adventures in the 8th grade

STONE ARCH BOOKS
a capstone imprint

STONE ARCH BOOKS™
Published in 2013
A Capstone Imprint
1710 Roe Crest Drive
North Mankato, MN 56003
www.capstonepub.com

Originally published by DC Comics in the U.S.
in single magazine form as Supergirl: Cosmic
Adventures in the 8th Grade #2.

Cataloging-in-Publication Data is available at the
Library of Congress website:
ISBN: 978-1-4342-4718-6 (library binding)

Summary: Superpowers should make life easier, but
they only seem to complicate things for Supergirl.
Life gets a lot crazier, though, when a new enemy
named Belinda Zee shows up. And with girls like
Belinda around, facing down Super-Villains doesn't
seem so bad.

STONE ARCH BOOKS
Ashley C. Andersen Zantop *Publisher*
Michael Dahl *Editorial Director*
Donald Lemke *Editor*
Heather Kindseth *Creative Director*
Brann Garvey *Designer*
Kathy McColley *Production Specialist*

DC COMICS
Jann Jones & Elisabeth V. Gehrlein *Original U.S. Editors*
Adam Schlagman *U.S. Associate Editor*
Simona Martore *U.S. Assistant Editor*
DC Comics
1700 Broadway, New York, NY 10019
A Warner Bros. Entertainment Company

Printed in China by Nordica.
1012/CA21201277
092012 006935NORDS13

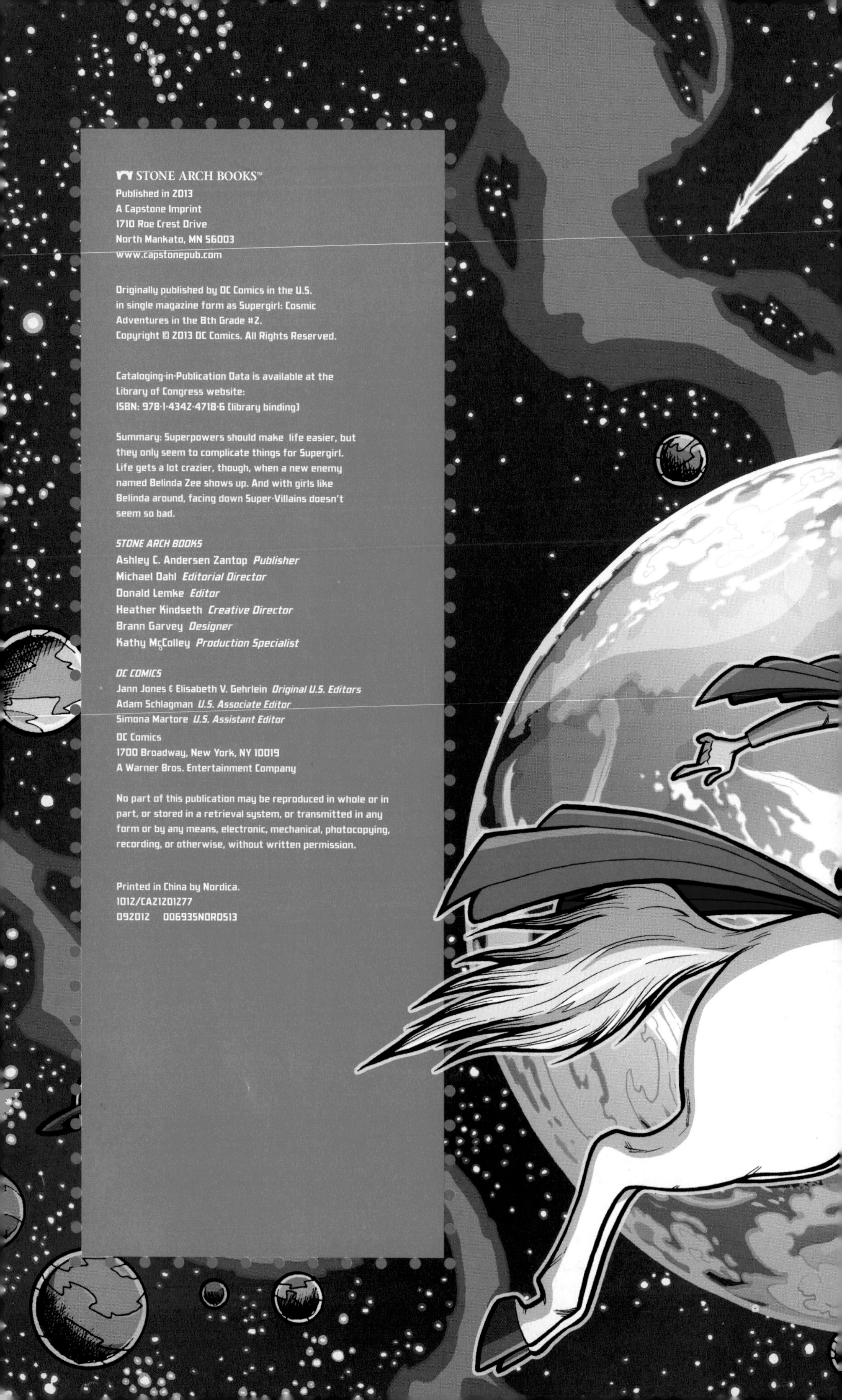

SuperGirl

cosmic adventures in the 8th grade

MY OWN BEST FRENEMY

LANDRY Q. WALKER
WRITER

ERIC JONES
ARTIST

JOEY MASON
COLORIST

PAT BROSSEAU
TRAVIS LANHAM
SAL CIPRIANO
LETTERERS

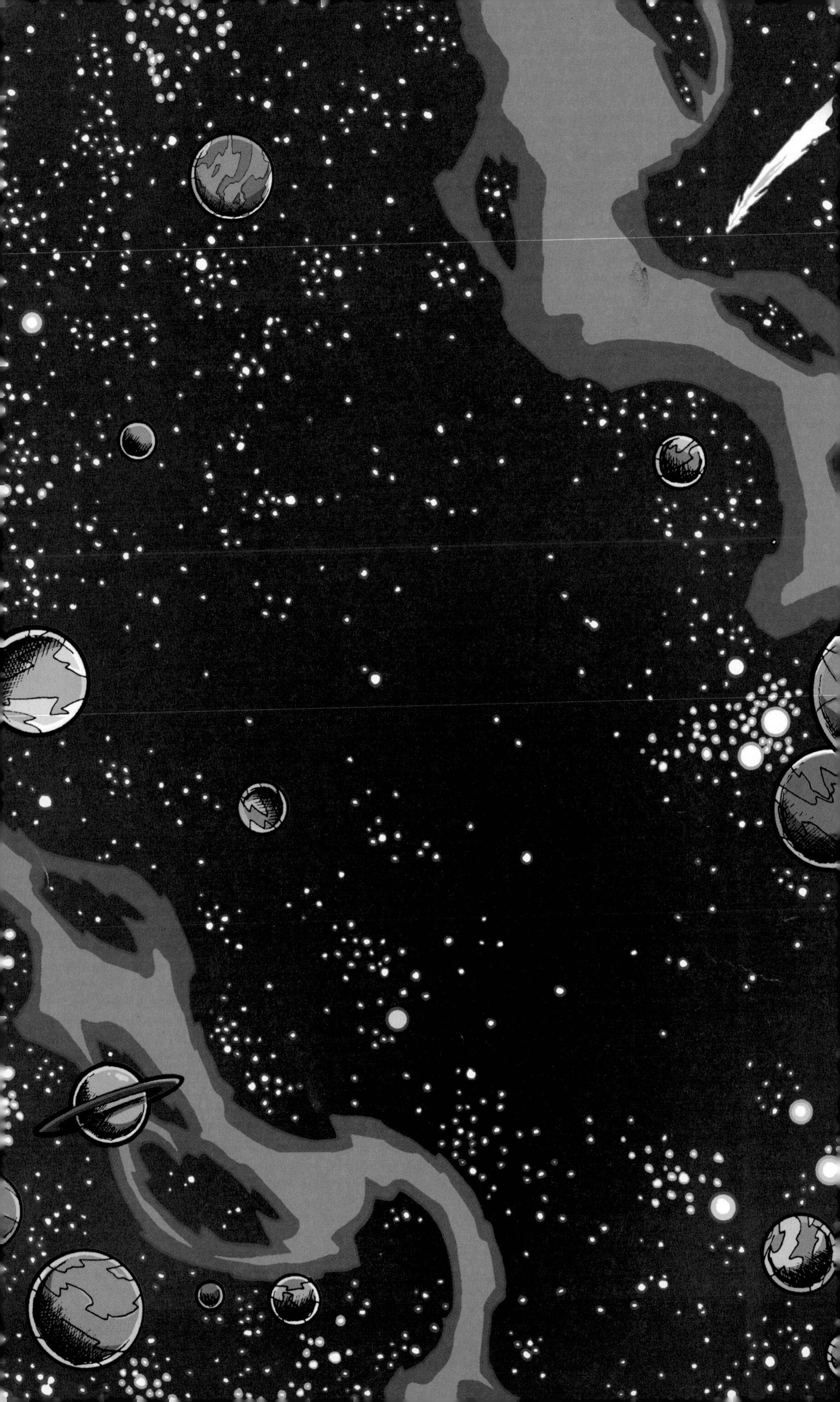

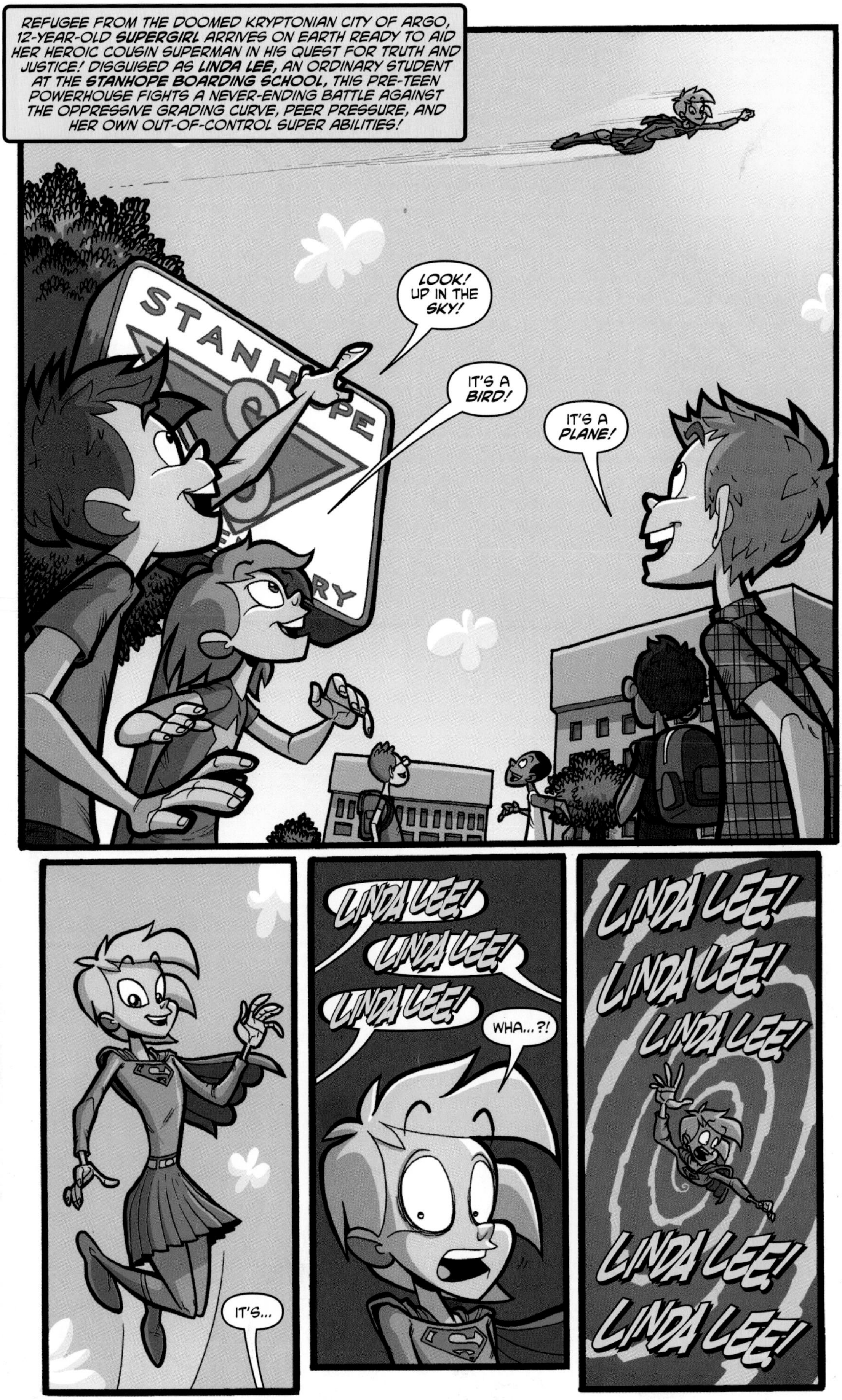
REFUGEE FROM THE DOOMED KRYPTONIAN CITY OF ARGO, 12-YEAR-OLD SUPERGIRL ARRIVES ON EARTH READY TO AID HER HEROIC COUSIN SUPERMAN IN HIS QUEST FOR TRUTH AND JUSTICE! DISGUISED AS LINDA LEE, AN ORDINARY STUDENT AT THE STANHOPE BOARDING SCHOOL, THIS PRE-TEEN POWERHOUSE FIGHTS A NEVER-ENDING BATTLE AGAINST THE OPPRESSIVE GRADING CURVE, PEER PRESSURE, AND HER OWN OUT-OF-CONTROL SUPER ABILITIES!
STANHOPE
LOOK! UP IN THE SKY!
IT'S A BIRD!
IT'S A PLANE!
IT'S...
LINDA LEE!
LINDA LEE!
LINDA LEE!
WHA...?!
LINDA LEE!
LINDA LEE!
LINDA LEE!
LINDA LEE!
LINDA LEE!

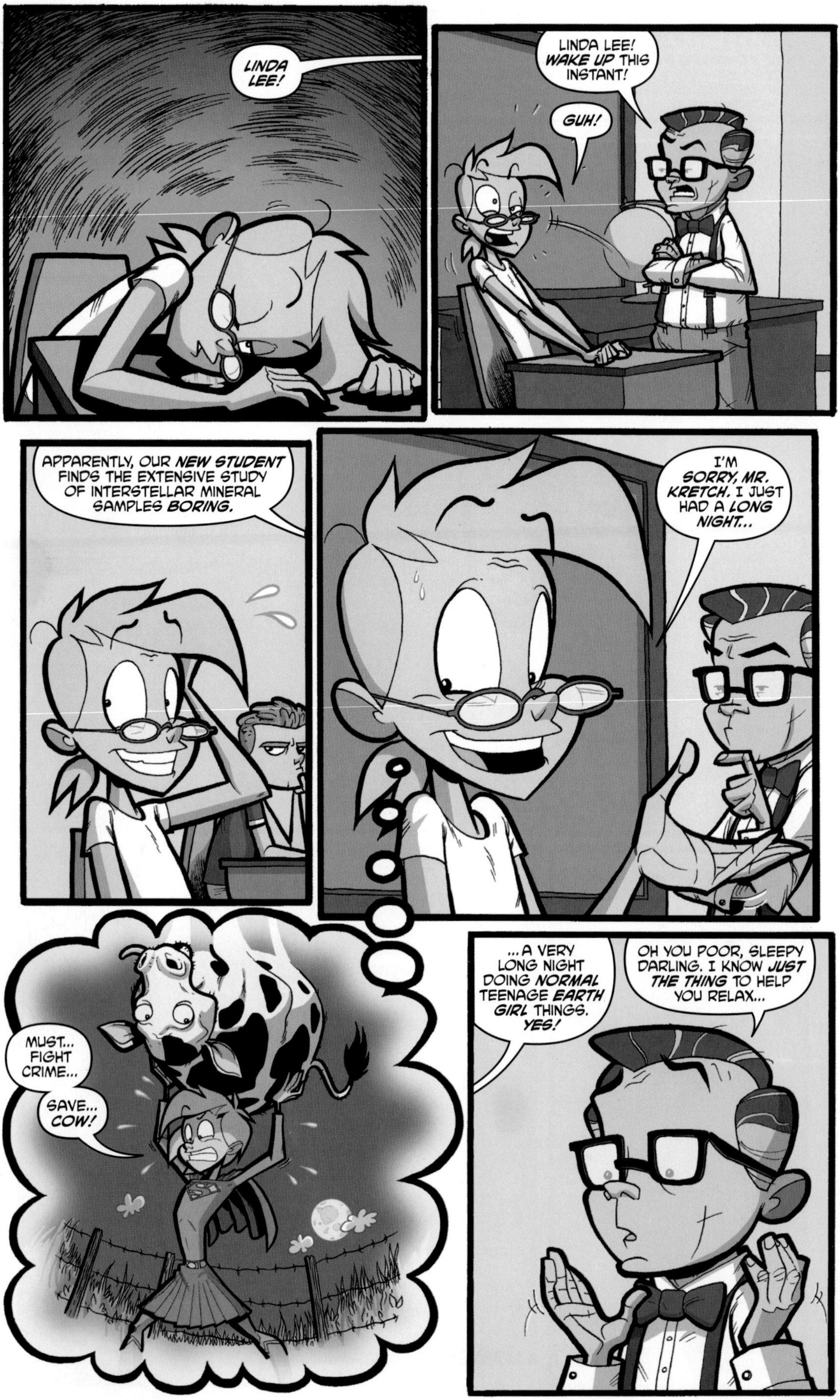
LINDA LEE!
LINDA LEE! WAKE UP THIS INSTANT!
GUH!
APPARENTLY, OUR NEW STUDENT FINDS THE EXTENSIVE STUDY OF INTERSTELLAR MINERAL SAMPLES BORING.
I'M SORRY, MR. KRETCH. I JUST HAD A LONG NIGHT...
MUST... FIGHT CRIME...
SAVE... COW!
...A VERY LONG NIGHT DOING NORMAL TEENAGE EARTH GIRL THINGS. YES!
OH YOU POOR, SLEEPY DARLING. I KNOW JUST THE THING TO HELP YOU RELAX...

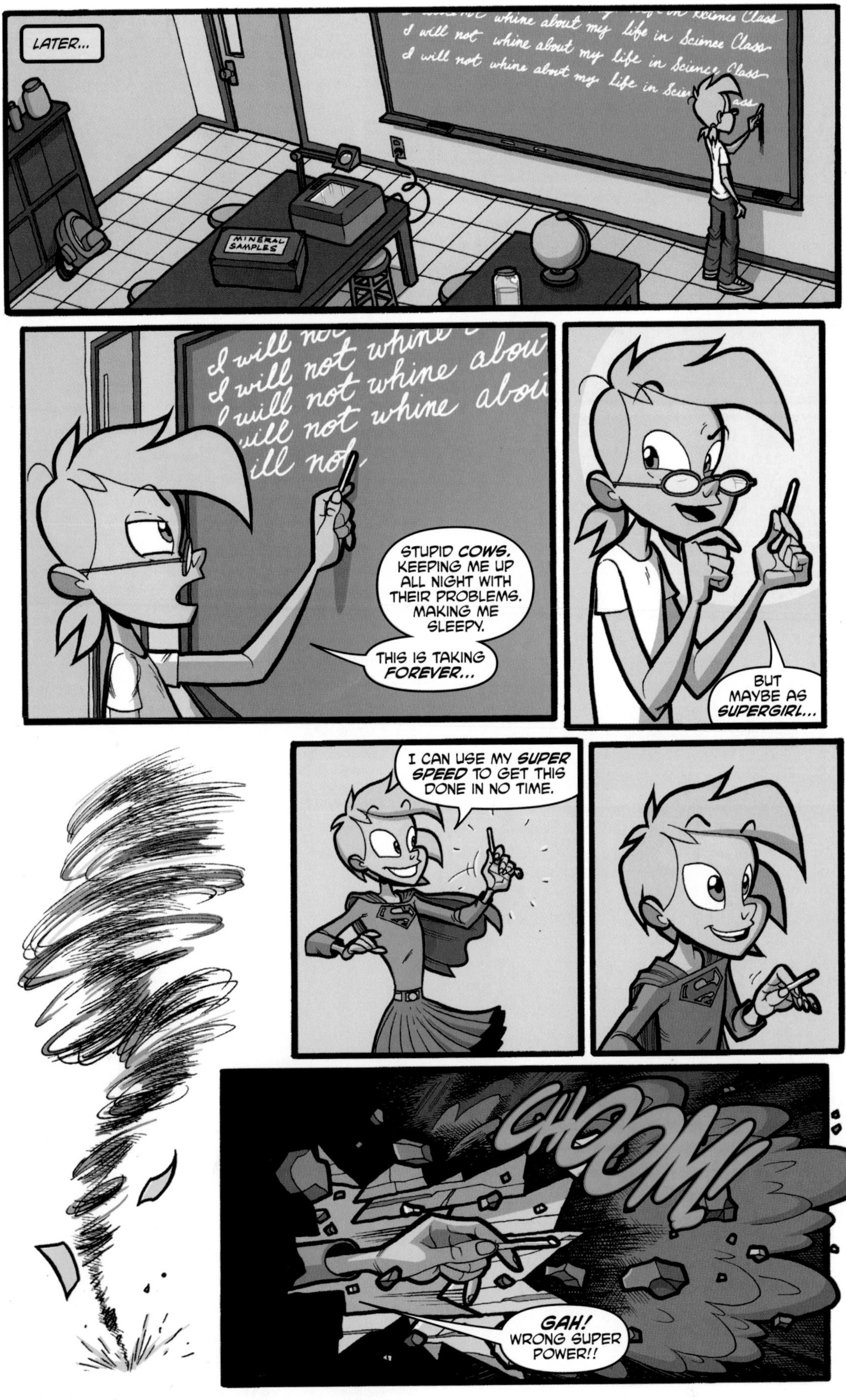
LATER...
I will not whine about my life in Science Class
I will not whine about my life in Science Class
I will not whine about my life in Science Class
MINERAL SAMPLES
STUPID COWS. KEEPING ME UP ALL NIGHT WITH THEIR PROBLEMS. MAKING ME SLEEPY.
THIS IS TAKING FOREVER...
BUT MAYBE AS SUPERGIRL...
I CAN USE MY SUPER SPEED TO GET THIS DONE IN NO TIME.
CHOOM!
GAH! WRONG SUPER POWER!!

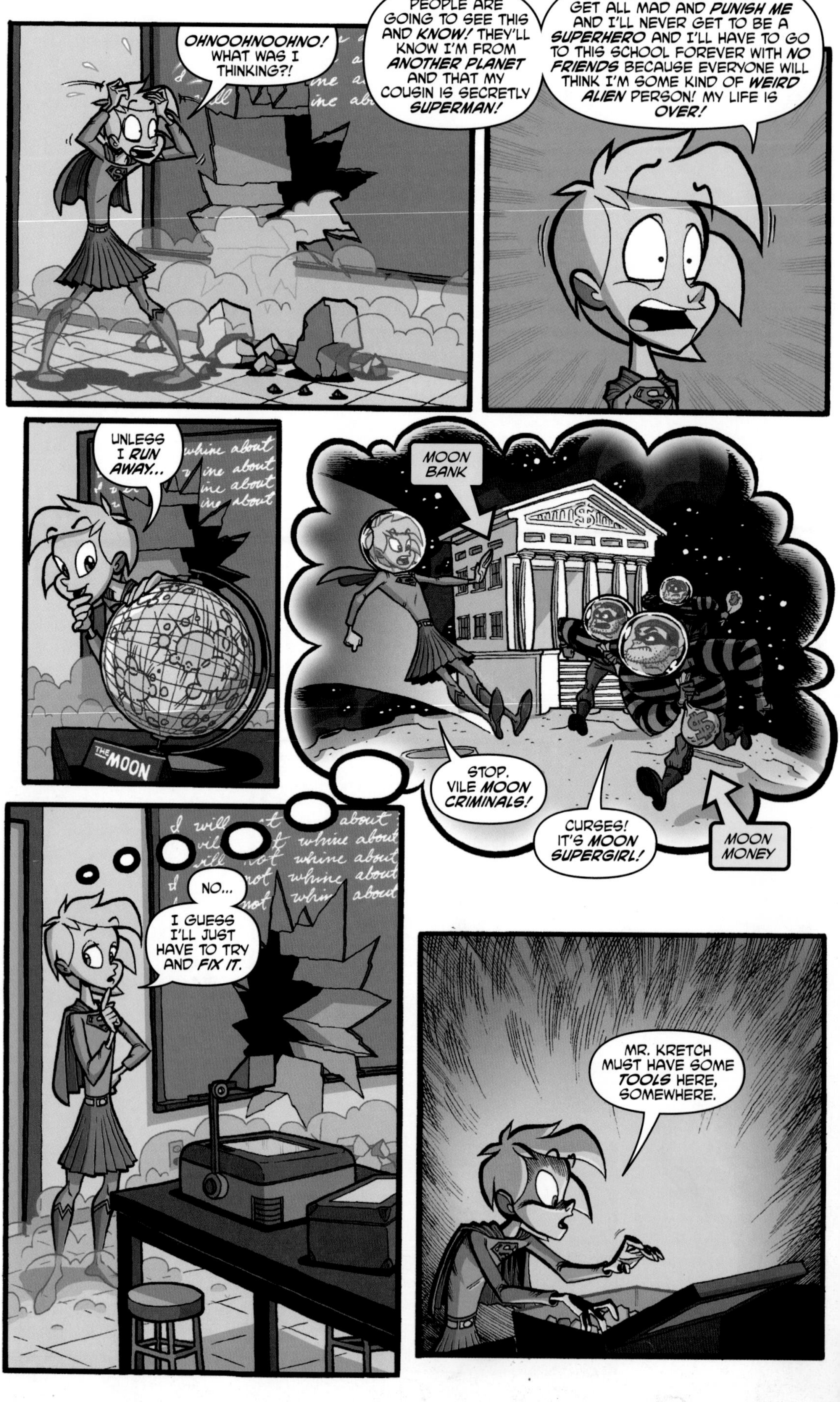
OHNOOHNOOHNO! WHAT WAS I THINKING?!
PEOPLE ARE GOING TO SEE THIS AND KNOW! THEY'LL KNOW I'M FROM ANOTHER PLANET AND THAT MY COUSIN IS SECRETLY SUPERMAN!
THEN SUPERMAN WILL GET ALL MAD AND PUNISH ME AND I'LL NEVER GET TO BE A SUPERHERO AND I'LL HAVE TO GO TO THIS SCHOOL FOREVER WITH NO FRIENDS BECAUSE EVERYONE WILL THINK I'M SOME KIND OF WEIRD ALIEN PERSON! MY LIFE IS OVER!
UNLESS I RUN AWAY...
THE MOON
MOON BANK
STOP. VILE MOON CRIMINALS!
CURSES! IT'S MOON SUPERGIRL!
MOON MONEY
NO...
I GUESS I'LL JUST HAVE TO TRY AND FIX IT.
MR. KRETCH MUST HAVE SOME TOOLS HERE, SOMEWHERE.

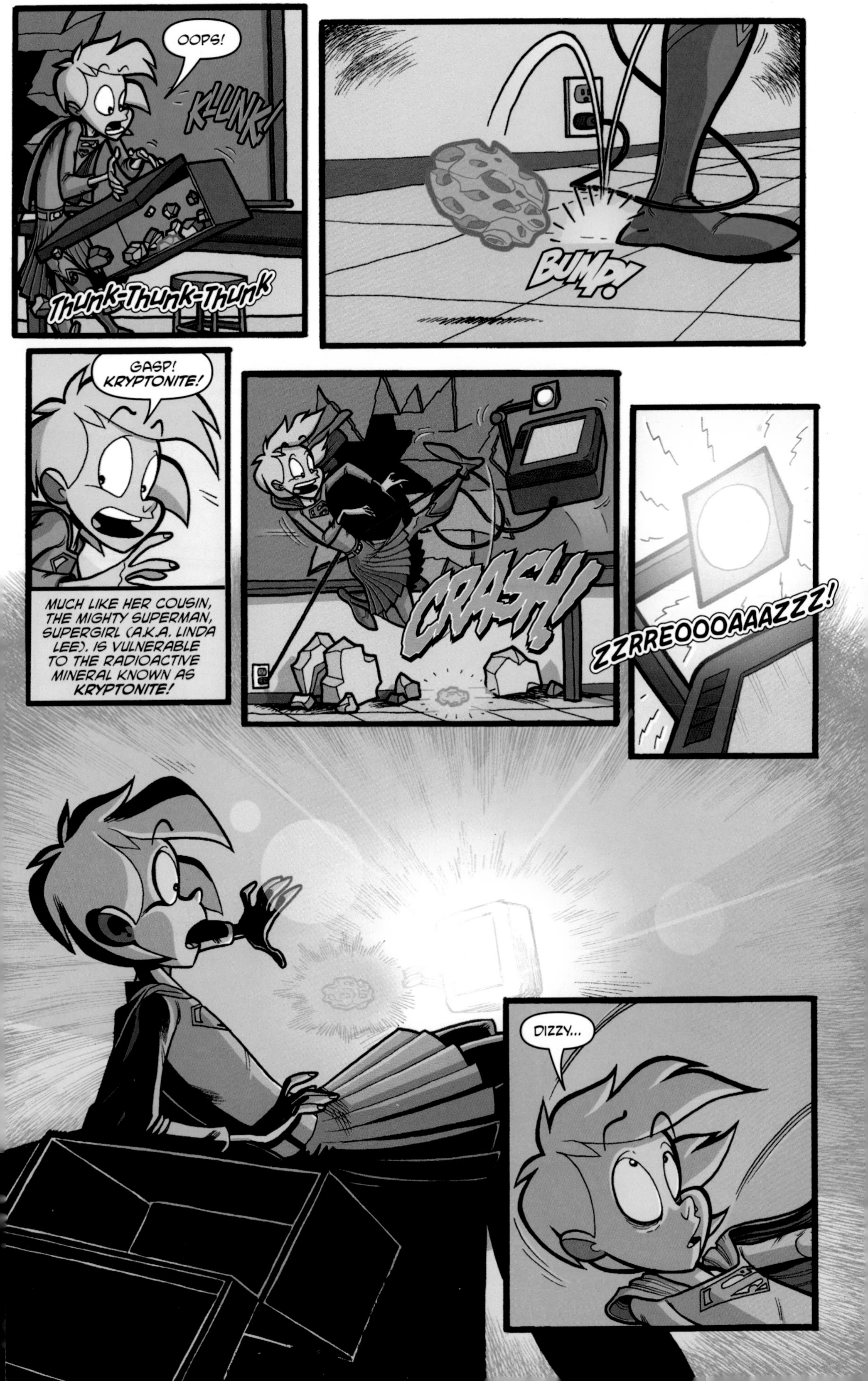
OOPS!
KLUNK!
THUNK-THUNK-THUNK
BUMP!
GASP! KRYPTONITE!
MUCH LIKE HER COUSIN, THE MIGHTY SUPERMAN, SUPERGIRL (A.K.A. LINDA LEE), IS VULNERABLE TO THE RADIOACTIVE MINERAL KNOWN AS KRYPTONITE!
CRASH!
ZZRREOOOAAAZZZ!
DIZZY...

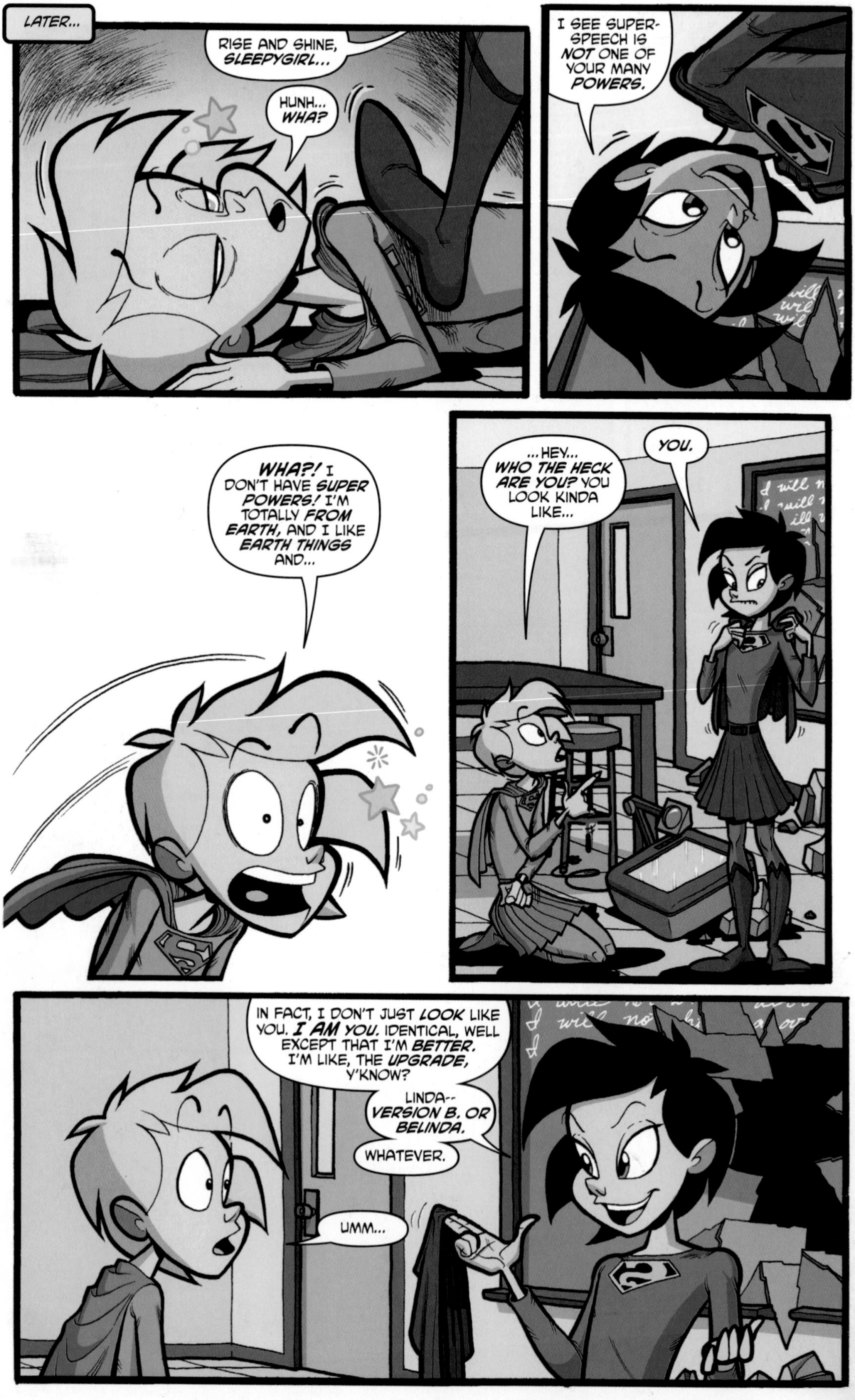

LATER...
RISE AND SHINE, SLEEPYGIRL...
HUNH... WHA?
I SEE SUPER-SPEECH IS NOT ONE OF YOUR MANY POWERS.
WHA?! I DON'T HAVE SUPER POWERS! I'M TOTALLY FROM EARTH, AND I LIKE EARTH THINGS AND...
...HEY... WHO THE HECK ARE YOU? YOU LOOK KINDA LIKE...
YOU.
IN FACT, I DON'T JUST LOOK LIKE YOU. I AM YOU. IDENTICAL, WELL EXCEPT THAT I'M BETTER. I'M LIKE, THE UPGRADE, Y'KNOW?
LINDA--VERSION B. OR BELINDA.
WHATEVER.
UMM...

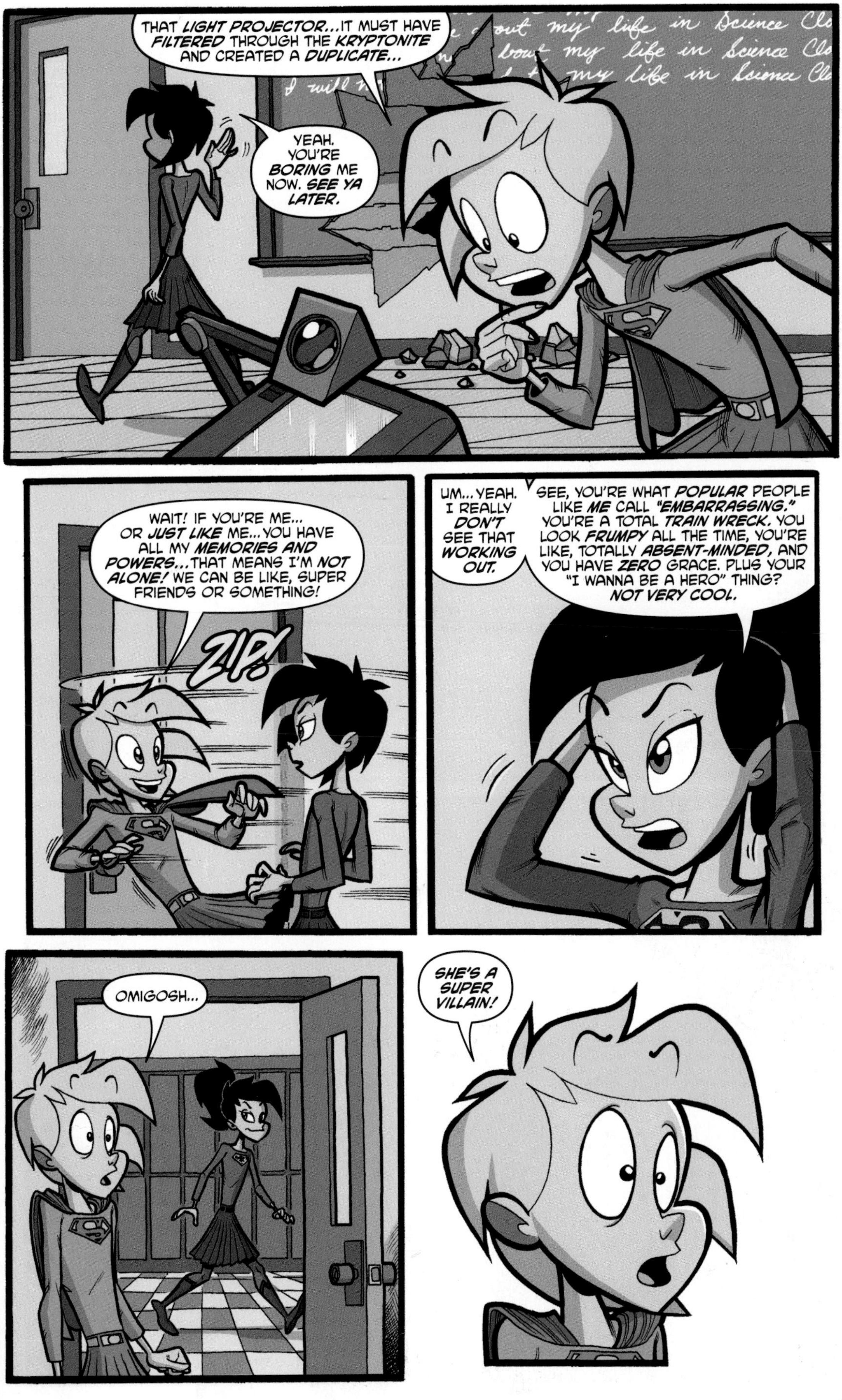
THAT LIGHT PROJECTOR...IT MUST HAVE FILTERED THROUGH THE KRYPTONITE AND CREATED A DUPLICATE...
YEAH. YOU'RE BORING ME NOW. SEE YA LATER.
WAIT! IF YOU'RE ME... OR JUST LIKE ME...YOU HAVE ALL MY MEMORIES AND POWERS...THAT MEANS I'M NOT ALONE! WE CAN BE LIKE, SUPER FRIENDS OR SOMETHING!
ZIP!
UM...YEAH. I REALLY DON'T SEE THAT WORKING OUT.
SEE, YOU'RE WHAT POPULAR PEOPLE LIKE ME CALL "EMBARRASSING." YOU'RE A TOTAL TRAIN WRECK. YOU LOOK FRUMPY ALL THE TIME, YOU'RE LIKE, TOTALLY ABSENT-MINDED, AND YOU HAVE ZERO GRACE. PLUS YOUR "I WANNA BE A HERO" THING? NOT VERY COOL.
OMIGOSH...
SHE'S A SUPER VILLAIN!

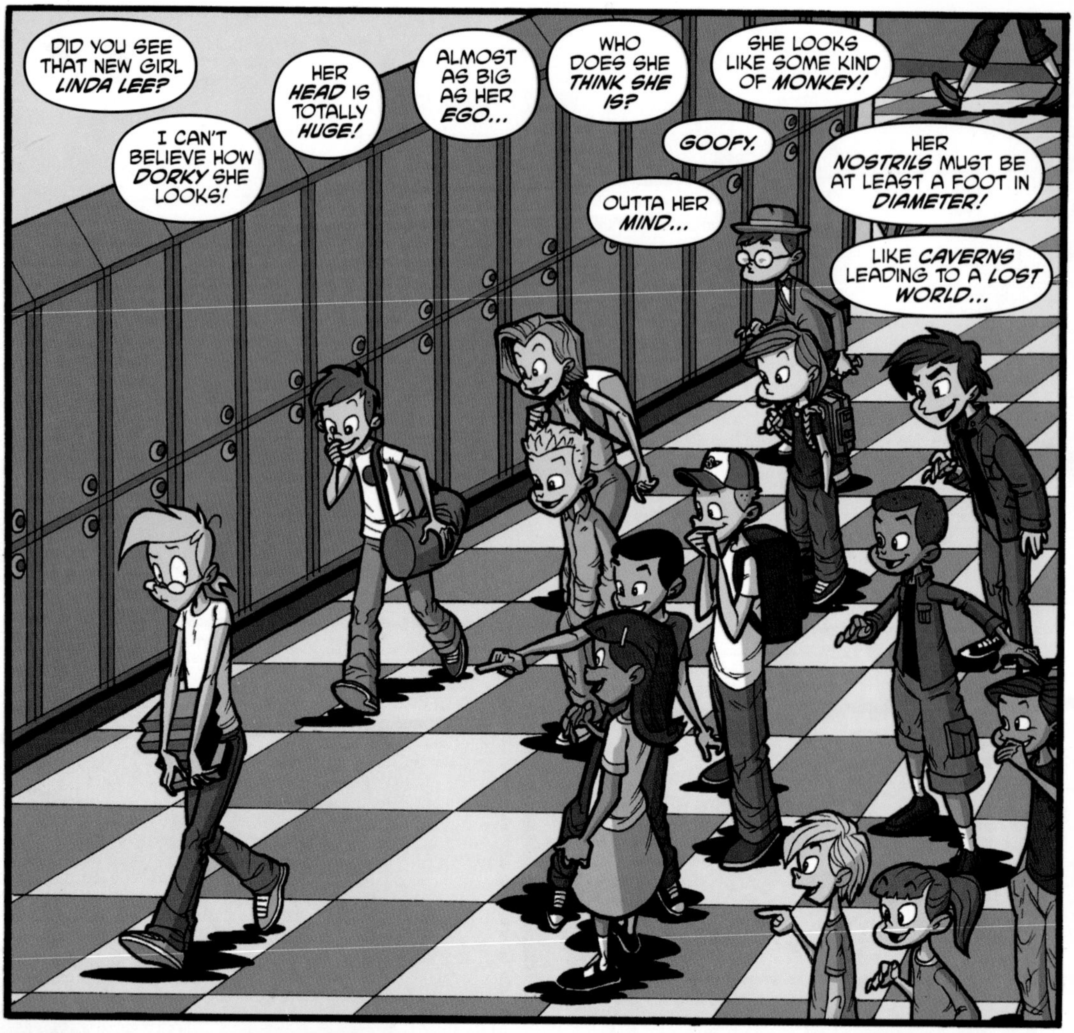

DID YOU SEE THAT NEW GIRL LINDA LEE?
I CAN'T BELIEVE HOW DORKY SHE LOOKS!
HER HEAD IS TOTALLY HUGE!
ALMOST AS BIG AS HER EGO...
WHO DOES SHE THINK SHE IS?
GOOFY.
OUTTA HER MIND...
SHE LOOKS LIKE SOME KIND OF MONKEY!
HER NOSTRILS MUST BE AT LEAST A FOOT IN DIAMETER!
LIKE CAVERNS LEADING TO A LOST WORLD...

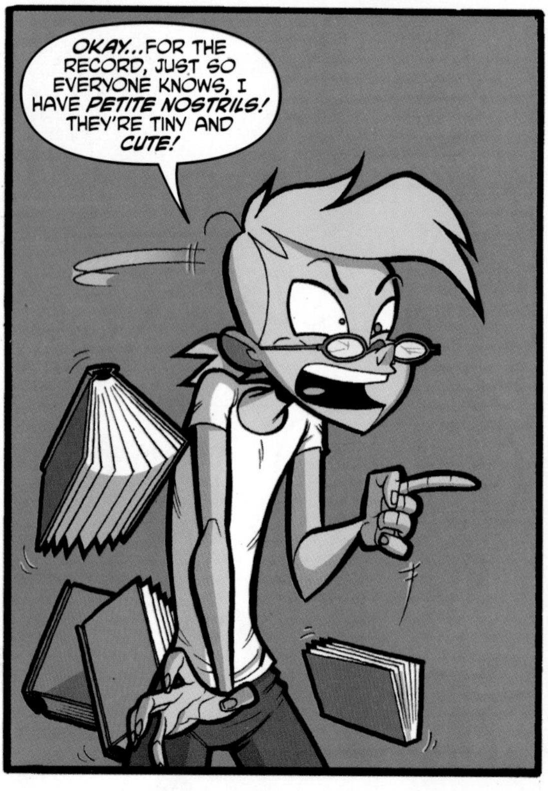

OKAY...FOR THE RECORD, JUST SO EVERYONE KNOWS, I HAVE PETITE NOSTRILS! THEY'RE TINY AND CUTE!

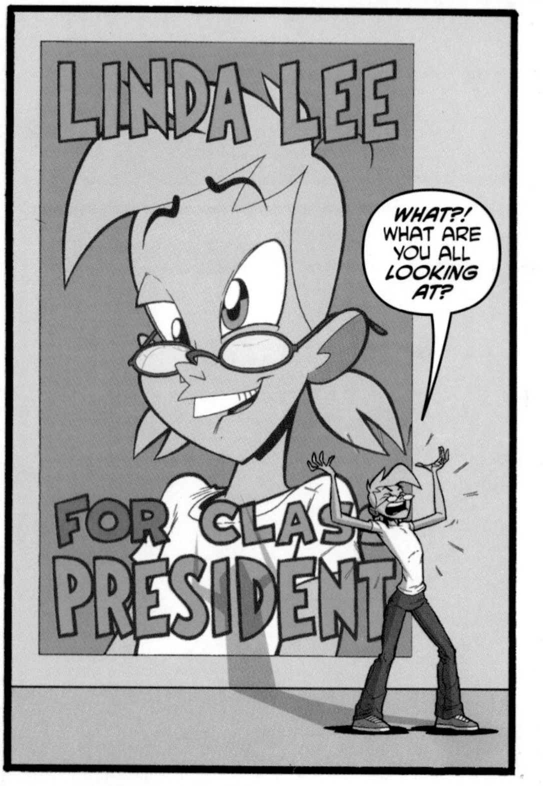

LINDA LEE
FOR CLAS
PRESIDENT
WHAT?! WHAT ARE YOU ALL LOOKING AT?

LINDA LEE FOR CLASS PRESIDENT
OH.
IT REALLY SEEMS TO CAPTURE THE *INNER YOU.*
AND CHECK OUT MY SECRET IDENTITY! CAPTAIN OF THE CHEERLEADERS. FREAKIN' AWESOME.
DID *YOU* DO THIS? *YOU* DID THIS! *WHY DID YOU DO THIS?!*
WE'LL TALK LATER. RIGHT NOW, YOU SHOULD GET UP TO THE *ROOF.*
GAK!
KA-BOOO
BYE!
-OOO-
ZING!

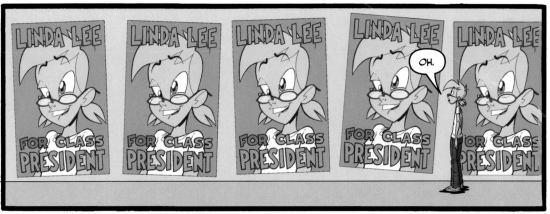

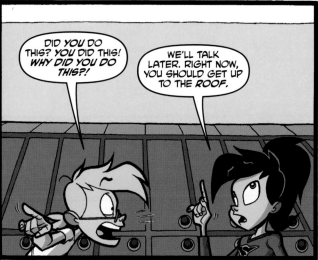

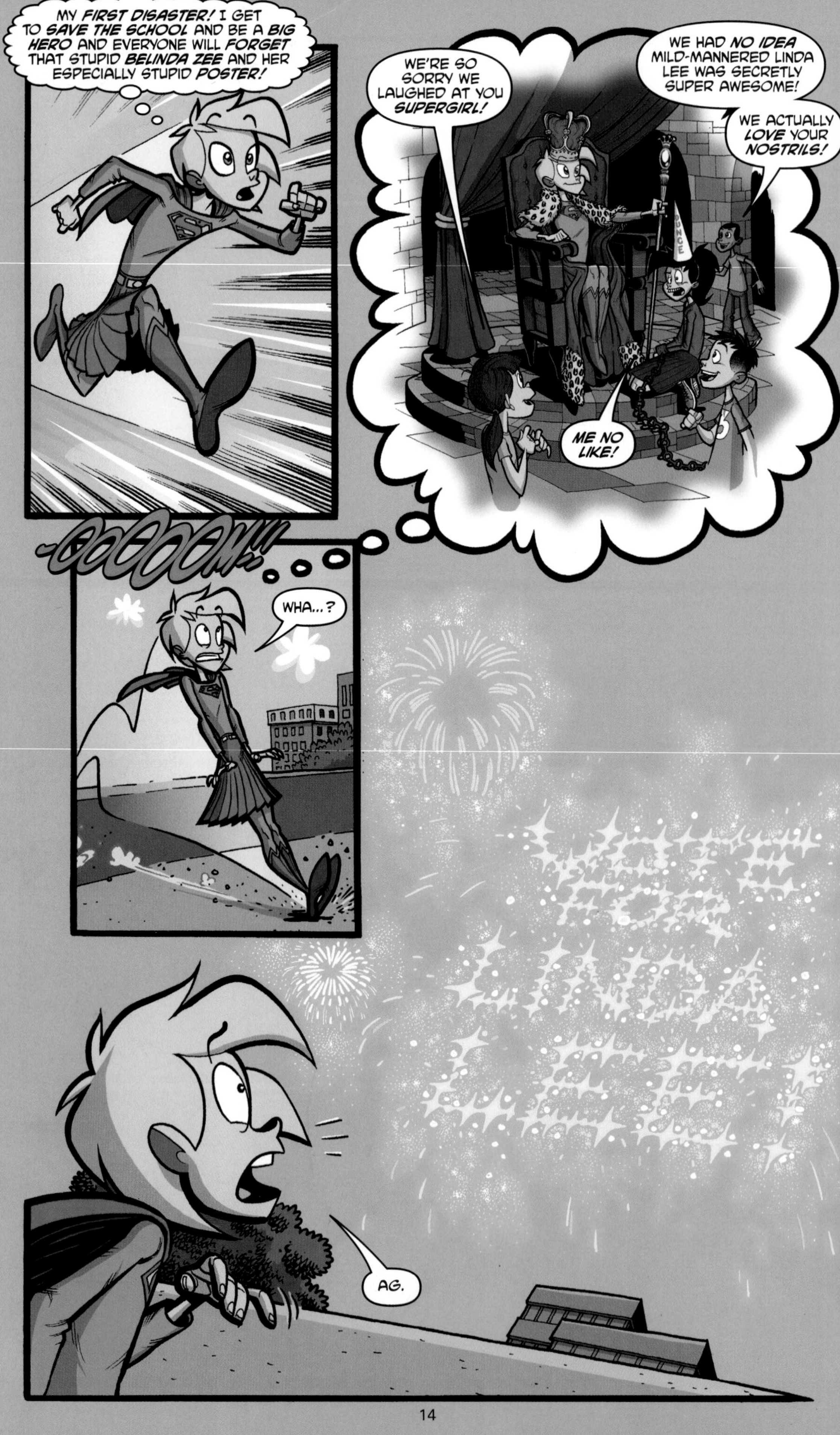
MY FIRST DISASTER! I GET TO SAVE THE SCHOOL AND BE A BIG HERO AND EVERYONE WILL FORGET THAT STUPID BELINDA ZEE AND HER ESPECIALLY STUPID POSTER!
WE'RE SO SORRY WE LAUGHED AT YOU SUPERGIRL!
WE HAD NO IDEA MILD-MANNERED LINDA LEE WAS SECRETLY SUPER AWESOME!
WE ACTUALLY LOVE YOUR NOSTRILS!
DUNCE
ME NO LIKE!
-OOOOOM!!!
WHA...?
AG.

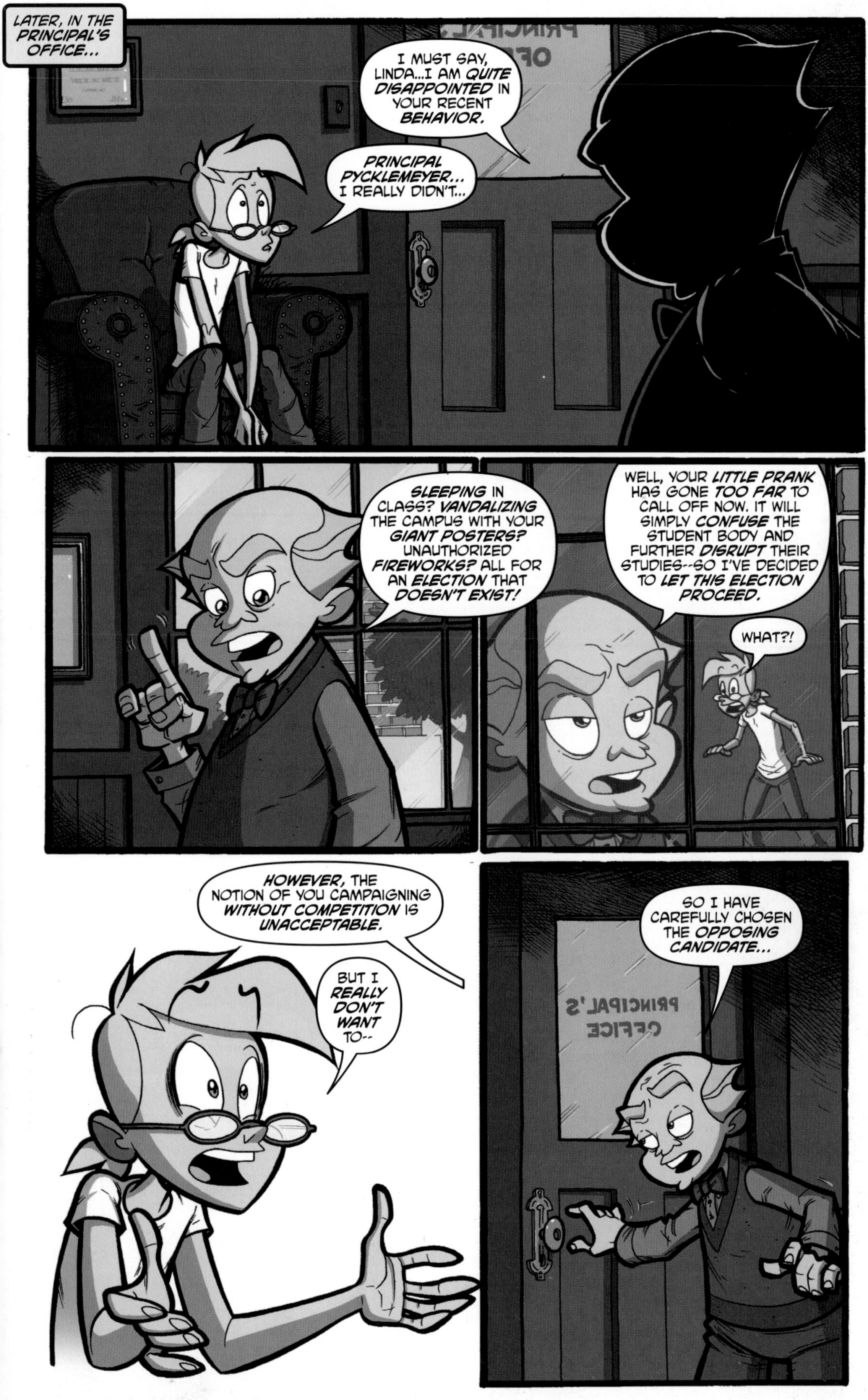
LATER, IN THE PRINCIPAL'S OFFICE...
PRINCIPAL'S OFFICE
I MUST SAY, LINDA...I AM QUITE DISAPPOINTED IN YOUR RECENT BEHAVIOR.
PRINCIPAL PYCKLEMEYER... I REALLY DIDN'T...
SLEEPING IN CLASS? VANDALIZING THE CAMPUS WITH YOUR GIANT POSTERS? UNAUTHORIZED FIREWORKS? ALL FOR AN ELECTION THAT DOESN'T EXIST!
WELL, YOUR LITTLE PRANK HAS GONE TOO FAR TO CALL OFF NOW. IT WILL SIMPLY CONFUSE THE STUDENT BODY AND FURTHER DISRUPT THEIR STUDIES--SO I'VE DECIDED TO LET THIS ELECTION PROCEED.
WHAT?!
HOWEVER, THE NOTION OF YOU CAMPAIGNING WITHOUT COMPETITION IS UNACCEPTABLE.
BUT I REALLY DON'T WANT TO--
SO I HAVE CAREFULLY CHOSEN THE OPPOSING CANDIDATE...
PRINCIPAL'S OFFICE

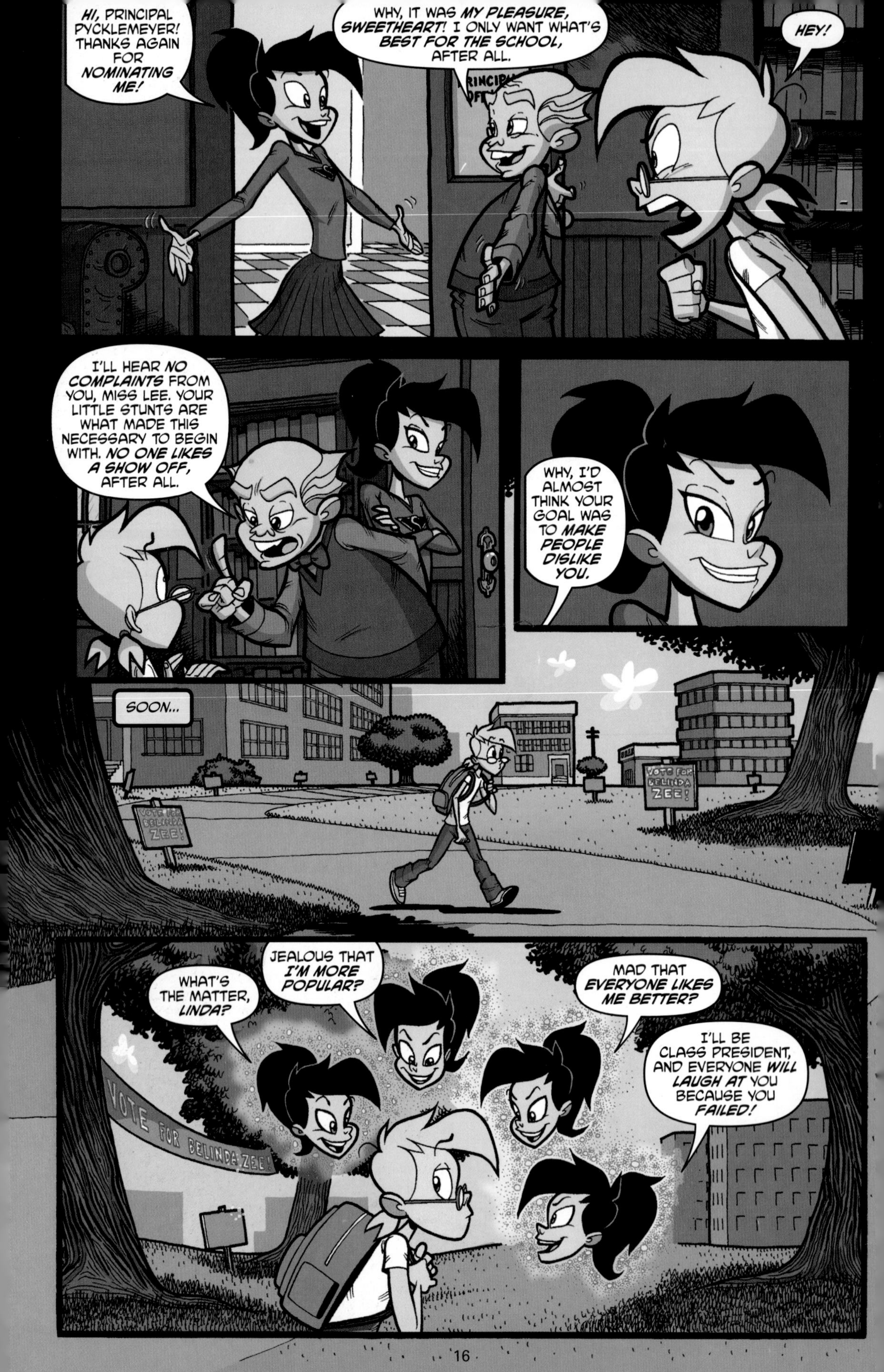
HI, PRINCIPAL PYCKLEMEYER! THANKS AGAIN FOR NOMINATING ME!
WHY, IT WAS MY PLEASURE, SWEETHEART! I ONLY WANT WHAT'S BEST FOR THE SCHOOL, AFTER ALL.
HEY!
I'LL HEAR NO COMPLAINTS FROM YOU, MISS LEE. YOUR LITTLE STUNTS ARE WHAT MADE THIS NECESSARY TO BEGIN WITH. NO ONE LIKES A SHOW OFF, AFTER ALL.
WHY, I'D ALMOST THINK YOUR GOAL WAS TO MAKE PEOPLE DISLIKE YOU.
SOON...
VOTE FOR BELINDA ZEE!
VOTE FOR BELINDA ZEE!
WHAT'S THE MATTER, LINDA?
JEALOUS THAT I'M MORE POPULAR?
MAD THAT EVERYONE LIKES ME BETTER?
I'LL BE CLASS PRESIDENT, AND EVERYONE WILL LAUGH AT YOU BECAUSE YOU FAILED!
VOTE FOR BELINDA ZEE!

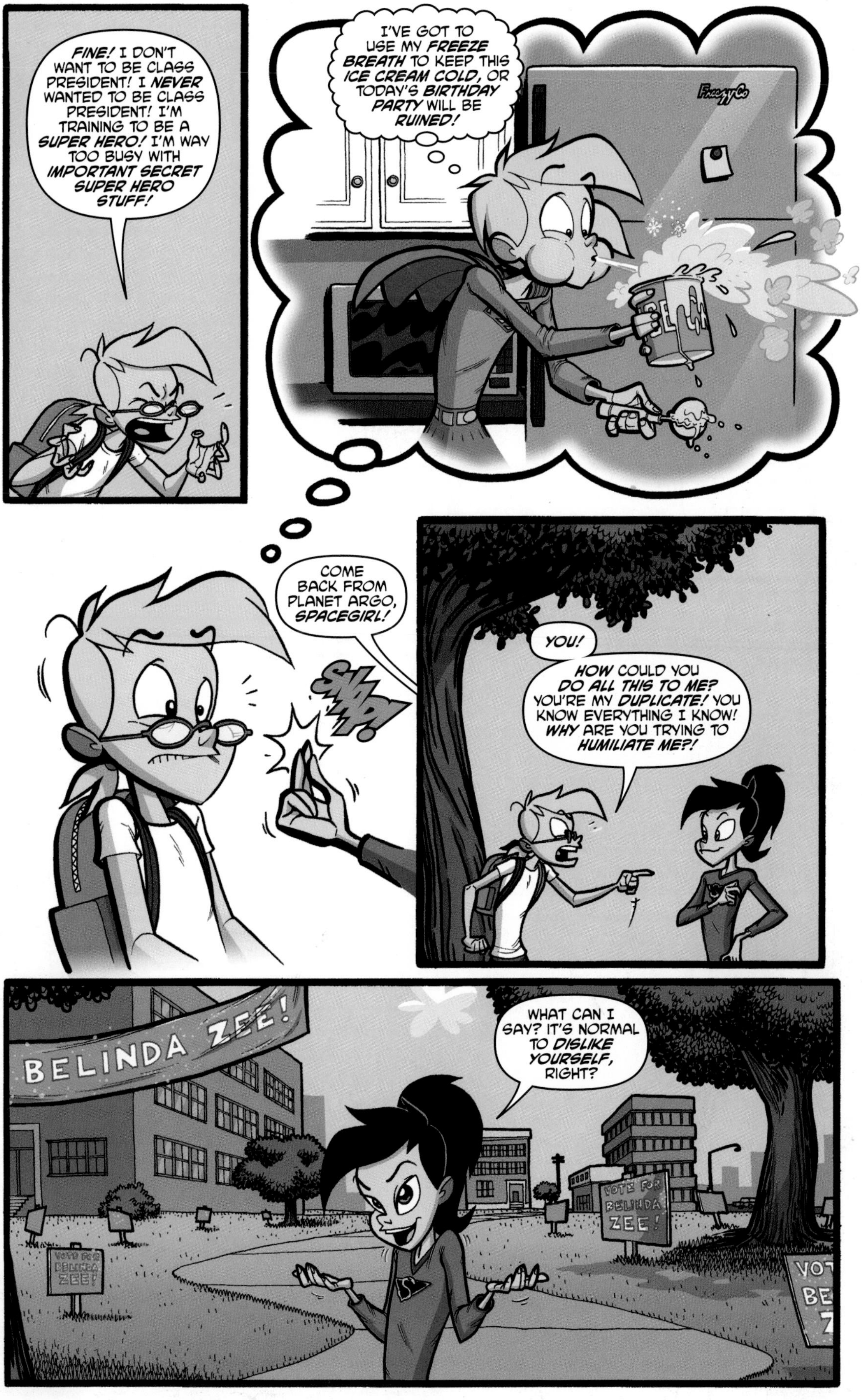
FINE! I DON'T WANT TO BE CLASS PRESIDENT! I NEVER WANTED TO BE CLASS PRESIDENT! I'M TRAINING TO BE A SUPER HERO! I'M WAY TOO BUSY WITH IMPORTANT SECRET SUPER HERO STUFF!
I'VE GOT TO USE MY FREEZE BREATH TO KEEP THIS ICE CREAM COLD, OR TODAY'S BIRTHDAY PARTY WILL BE RUINED!
COME BACK FROM PLANET ARGO, SPACEGIRL!
SNAP!
YOU!
HOW COULD YOU DO ALL THIS TO ME? YOU'RE MY DUPLICATE! YOU KNOW EVERYTHING I KNOW! WHY ARE YOU TRYING TO HUMILIATE ME?!
BELINDA ZEE!
WHAT CAN I SAY? IT'S NORMAL TO DISLIKE YOURSELF, RIGHT?
VOTE FOR BELINDA ZEE!

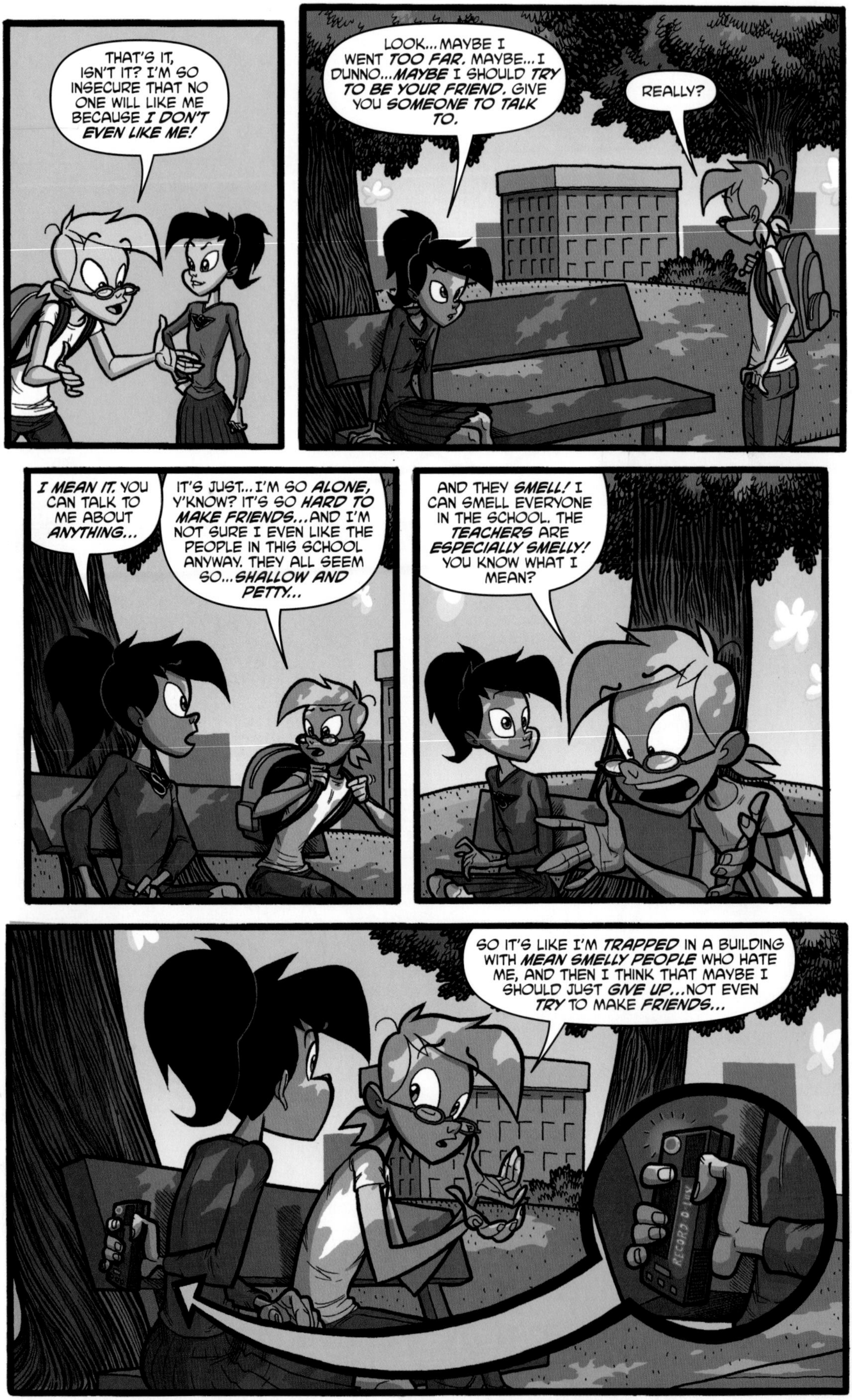
THAT'S IT, ISN'T IT? I'M SO INSECURE THAT NO ONE WILL LIKE ME BECAUSE *I DON'T EVEN LIKE ME!*
LOOK... MAYBE I WENT *TOO FAR.* MAYBE... I DUNNO... *MAYBE* I SHOULD *TRY TO BE YOUR FRIEND.* GIVE YOU *SOMEONE TO TALK TO.*
REALLY?
I MEAN IT. YOU CAN TALK TO ME ABOUT *ANYTHING...*
IT'S JUST... I'M SO *ALONE,* Y'KNOW? IT'S SO *HARD TO MAKE FRIENDS...* AND I'M NOT SURE I EVEN LIKE THE PEOPLE IN THIS SCHOOL ANYWAY. THEY ALL SEEM SO... *SHALLOW AND PETTY...*
AND THEY *SMELL!* I CAN SMELL EVERYONE IN THE SCHOOL. THE *TEACHERS* ARE *ESPECIALLY SMELLY!* YOU KNOW WHAT I MEAN?
SO IT'S LIKE I'M *TRAPPED* IN A BUILDING WITH *MEAN SMELLY PEOPLE* WHO HATE ME, AND THEN I THINK THAT MAYBE I SHOULD JUST *GIVE UP...* NOT EVEN *TRY* TO MAKE *FRIENDS...*

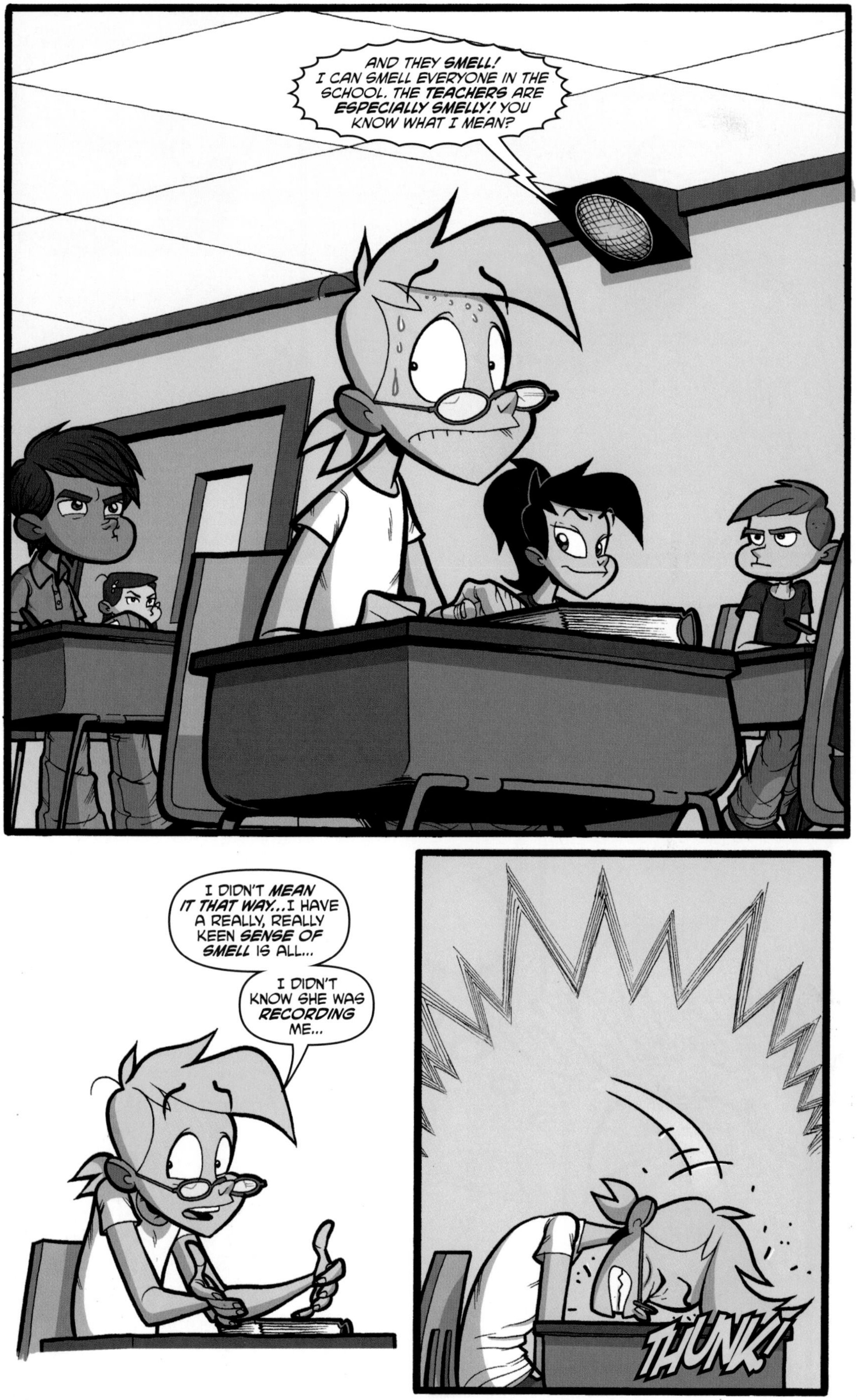
AND THEY SMELL! I CAN SMELL EVERYONE IN THE SCHOOL. THE TEACHERS ARE ESPECIALLY SMELLY! YOU KNOW WHAT I MEAN?
I DIDN'T MEAN IT THAT WAY...I HAVE A REALLY, REALLY KEEN SENSE OF SMELL IS ALL...
I DIDN'T KNOW SHE WAS RECORDING ME...
THUNK!

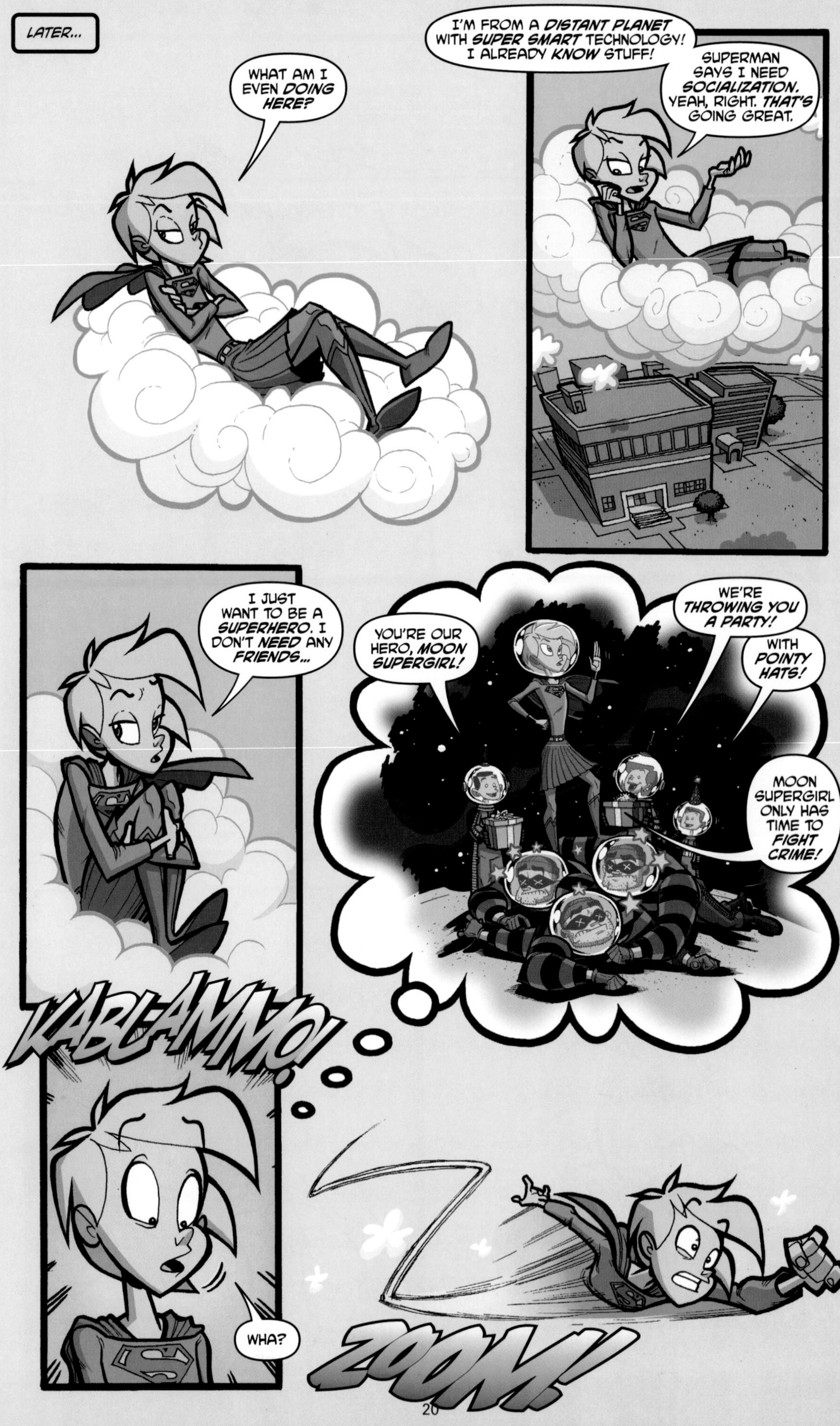
LATER...
WHAT AM I EVEN *DOING HERE?*
I'M FROM A *DISTANT PLANET* WITH *SUPER SMART* TECHNOLOGY! I ALREADY *KNOW* STUFF!
SUPERMAN SAYS I NEED *SOCIALIZATION.* YEAH, RIGHT. *THAT'S* GOING GREAT.
I JUST WANT TO BE A *SUPERHERO.* I DON'T *NEED* ANY *FRIENDS...*
YOU'RE OUR HERO, *MOON SUPERGIRL!*
WE'RE *THROWING YOU A PARTY!*
WITH *POINTY HATS!*
MOON SUPERGIRL ONLY HAS TIME TO *FIGHT CRIME!*
KABLAMMO!
WHA?
ZOOM!

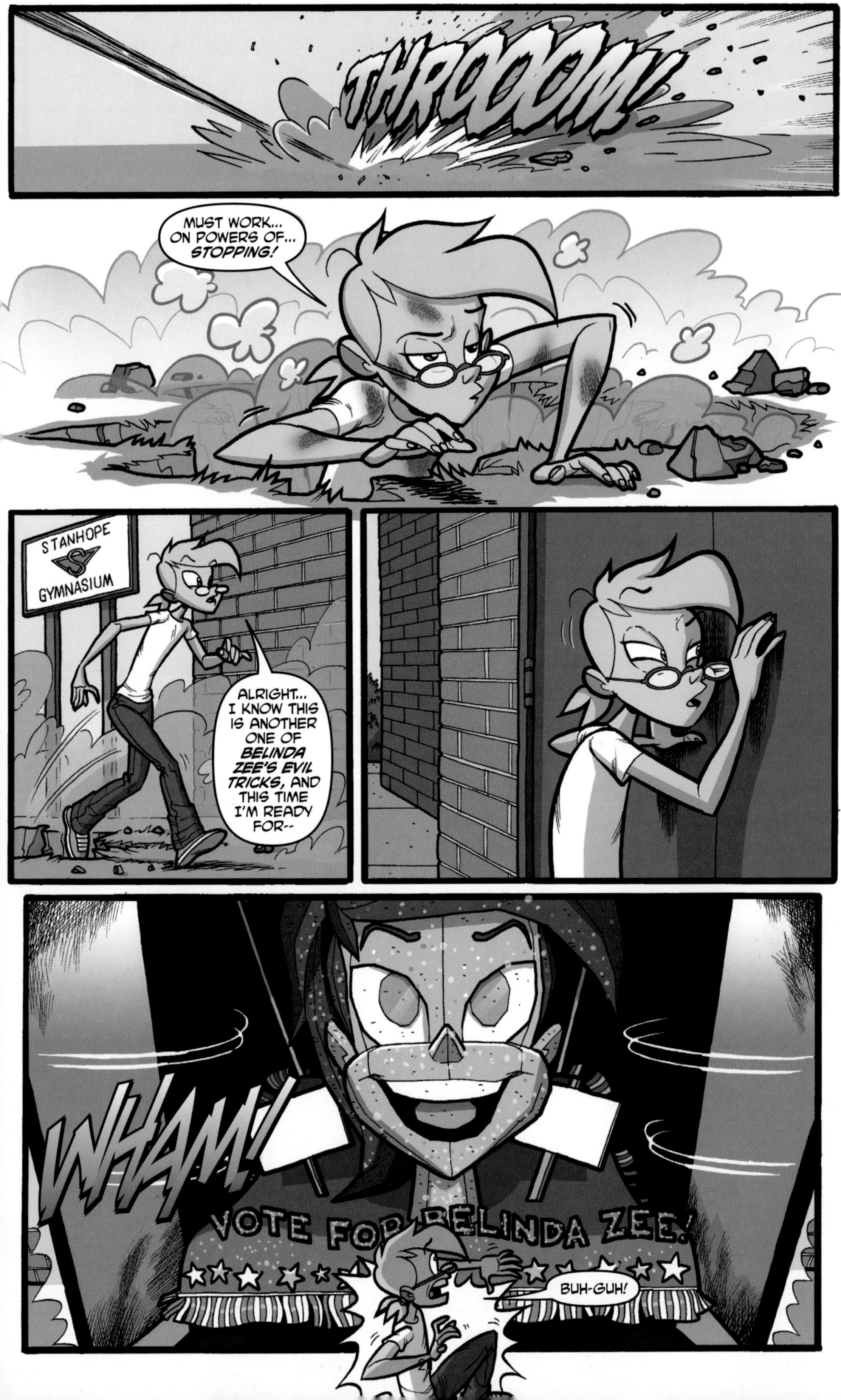
THROOOOM!
MUST WORK... ON POWERS OF... STOPPING!
STANHOPE GYMNASIUM
ALRIGHT... I KNOW THIS IS ANOTHER ONE OF BELINDA ZEE'S EVIL TRICKS, AND THIS TIME I'M READY FOR--
WHAM!
VOTE FOR BELINDA ZEE!
BUH-GUH!

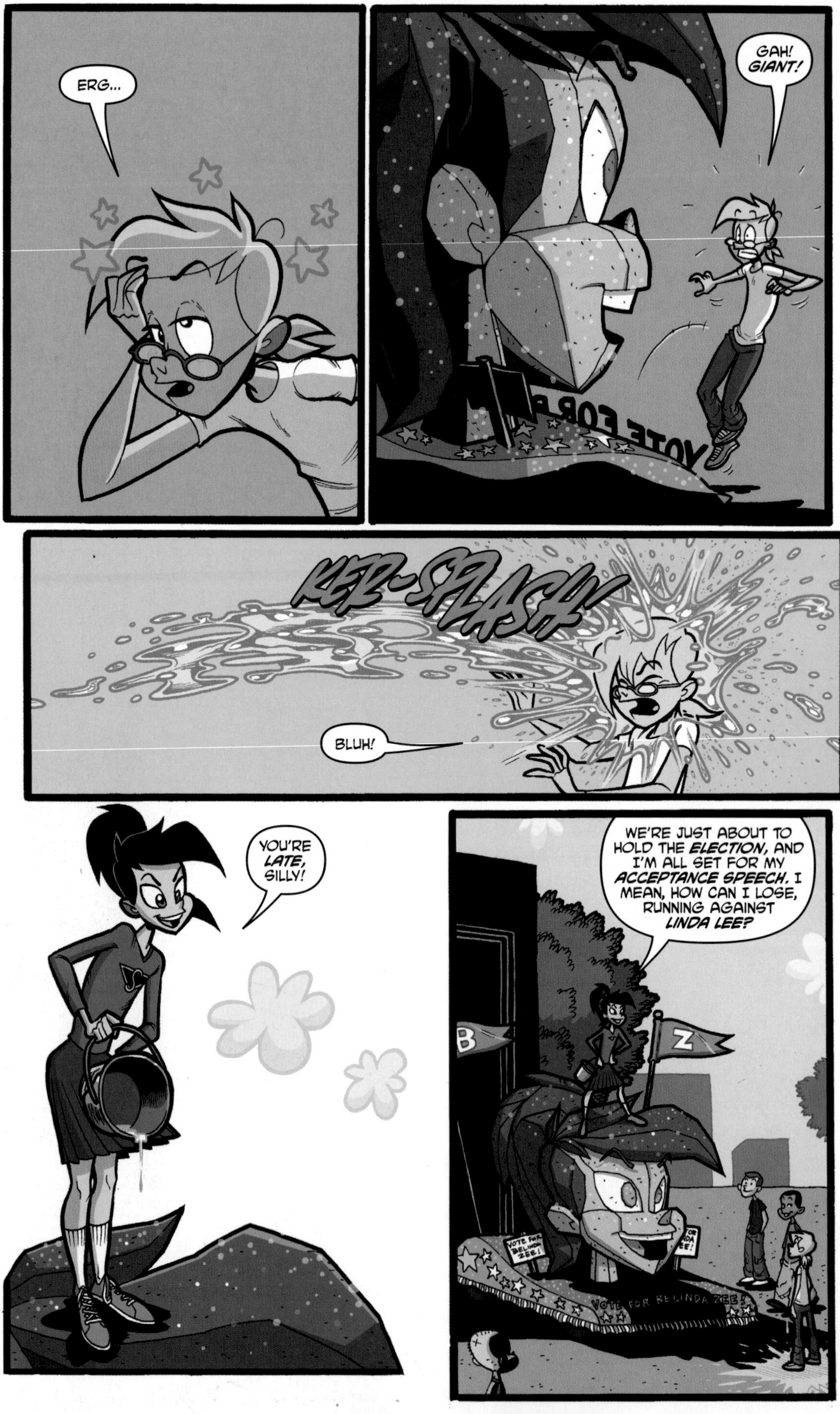
ERG...
GAH! GIANT!
VOTE FOR B
KER-SPLASH!
BLUH!
YOU'RE LATE, SILLY!
WE'RE JUST ABOUT TO HOLD THE ELECTION, AND I'M ALL SET FOR MY ACCEPTANCE SPEECH. I MEAN, HOW CAN I LOSE, RUNNING AGAINST LINDA LEE?
B
Z
VOTE FOR BELINDA ZEE!
VOTE FOR BELINDA ZEE!

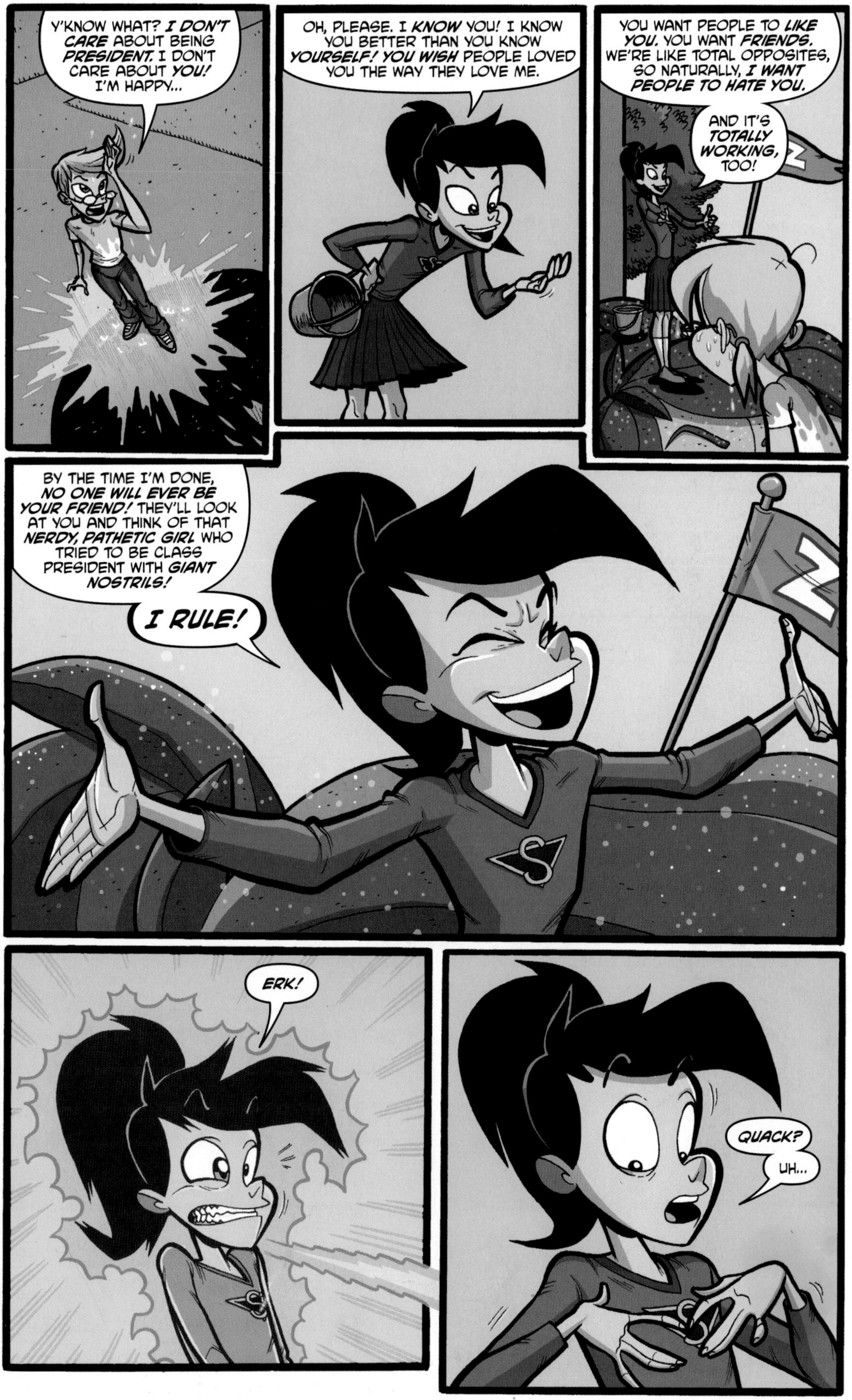
Y'KNOW WHAT? I DON'T CARE ABOUT BEING PRESIDENT. I DON'T CARE ABOUT YOU! I'M HAPPY...
OH, PLEASE. I KNOW YOU! I KNOW YOU BETTER THAN YOU KNOW YOURSELF! YOU WISH PEOPLE LOVED YOU THE WAY THEY LOVE ME.
YOU WANT PEOPLE TO LIKE YOU. YOU WANT FRIENDS. WE'RE LIKE TOTAL OPPOSITES, SO NATURALLY, I WANT PEOPLE TO HATE YOU.
AND IT'S TOTALLY WORKING, TOO!
BY THE TIME I'M DONE, NO ONE WILL EVER BE YOUR FRIEND! THEY'LL LOOK AT YOU AND THINK OF THAT NERDY, PATHETIC GIRL WHO TRIED TO BE CLASS PRESIDENT WITH GIANT NOSTRILS!
I RULE!
ERK!
QUACK?
UH...

QUACK! QUACK! QUACK!

QUACK!

QUACK!

QUACK!

QUACK!

VOTE FOR BELINDA ZEE!

BELINDA ZEE #1!

VOTE FOR BELINDA ZEE

OKAY. THE PLANET EARTH *OFFICIALLY* SCARES ME.

THAT'S A *WEIRD THING* TO SAY.

UH...IT'S AN EXPRESSION FROM...*KANSAS,* MY VERY *NORMAL* HOMETOWN.

AH.

DO YOU KNOW WHY EVERYONE THINKS THEY'RE *DUCKS?*

YEAH...UH. THAT WAS SORTA *MY FAULT.* I BUILT THIS *MIND CONTROL HELMET* THING BUT IT DOESN'T WORK RIGHT. IT MAKES PEOPLE *THINK THEY'RE DUCKS.*

I'M LENA. *LENA THORUL.*

I'M LINDA. *LINDA LEE.*

YEAH, I KNOW. WE'RE IN *SCIENCE* TOGETHER. AND I SAW THE *GIANT SCARY POSTER* OF YOU IN THE HALL.

THAT'S KINDA WHY I BUILT THE *MIND-CONTROL-ACCIDENTAL-DUCK MACHINE.*

EVERYONE WAS BEING *REALLY MEAN TO YOU,* ESPECIALLY THAT *CHEERLEADER* GIRL. AND *WE'RE BOTH NEW* HERE, AND I THOUGHT MAYBE WE *SHOULD BE FRIENDS,* AND IF YOU WERE GOING TO BE MY FRIEND, I DIDN'T WANT PEOPLE BEING MEAN TO YOU.

OH.

SO I BUILT THIS. I'M A LITTLE BIT OF A *SCIENCE TECH NERD.*

SO DO YOU WANNA BE *FRIENDS?*

UM... *YEAH.* YEAH, I DO.

WILL THEY ALL *STOP BEING DUCKS?*

I THINK SO. *MAYBE.*

LATER...

This has been the craziest week.

I'm not really popular. It's hard to fit in to this culture. No one really liked me much at first.

But now I have a new best friend. She's kinda nerdy (in a good way) and she likes helping people like me, and we even managed to get into the same dorm room.

I made my first super enemy. An evil doppelganger of me. She's a cheerleader, and really popular, and a jerk.

✉ Send

From: LINDA LEE ▼
To: SUPERMAN
Subject: The usual ramblings...

This has been the crazi... week. ...really popular. It's hard t... it in to th... ...No one really liked me much... ...enemy. An evil... She's a cheerle... d a jerk...

For the first time, I feel like I'll be okay on this planet. Anyway, I hope you visit soon.

Love, Linda.

KLICK

This has been the craziest week. I'm not really popular. It's hard to fit in to this culture. No one really liked me much at first. I made my first super enemy. An evil doppelganger of me. She's a cheerleader, and really popular, and a jerk.

I finally feel settled in.

The school is kinda weird. Science class is too easy, and the teachers are dumb.

But I have a best friend now. You'd like her. She's not at all like the regular people of Metropolis.

I wish I could come visit you in prison. But I know we have to watch out for that stupid Superman until the time is right. I can't tell you how much I hate him for making my big brother out to be a criminal.

Anyway, you take care and thanks again for sending me here to the Stanhope Boarding School. I miss you.

Love, Lena.

Send

From: LENA THORUL

To: LEX LUTHOR

Subject: re:Revenge!!!!

I wish I could come visit prison. But I know we have watch out for that stupid Superman until the time is I can't tell you how much I him for making my big br to be a criminal.

Anyway, you take care and again for sending me here Stanhope Boarding School. I miss you.

Love, Lena.

KLIK

NIGHT, LENA.

NIGHT, LINDA.

CREATORS

LANDRY Q. WALKER WRITER

Landry Q. Walker is a comics writer whose projects include *Supergirl: Cosmic Adventures in the 8th Grade* and more. He has also written *Batman: The Brave and the Bold*, the comic book adventures of The Incredibles, and contributed stories to *Disney Adventures* magazine and the gaming website Elder-Geek.

ERIC JONES ARTIST

Eric Jones is a professional comic book artist whose work for DC Comics include *Batman: The Brave and the Bold*, *Supergirl: Cosmic Adventures in the 8th Grade*, *Cartoon Network Action Pack*, and more.

JOEY MASON COLORIST

Joey Mason is an illustrator, animation artist, and comic book colorist. His work for DC Comics include *Supergirl: Cosmic Adventures in the 8th Grade*, as well as set designs for *Green Lantern: The Animated Series*.

GLOSSARY

diameter [dye·AM·uh·tur]—a straight line through the center of a circle, from one side to another

duplicate [DOO·pluh·kit]—an exact copy of something

humiliate [hyoo·MIL·ee·ate]—to make someone look or feel foolish or embarrassed

insecure [in·si·KYOOR]—not confident or sure

Kryptonite [KRIP·tuh·nite]—a radioactive material from the planet Krypton, able to weaken the superpowers of Superman and Supergirl

peer [PIHR]—an equal, or a person of the same age, rank, or standing as another

petite [puh·TEET]—having a small trim figure

petty [PET·ee]—trivial or unimportant

refugee [ref·yuh·JEE]—a person who is forced to leave his or her home because of war, persecution, or a natural disaster

vulnerable [VUHL·nur·uh·buhl]—in a weak position or mental state and likely to be hurt

VISUAL QUESTIONS & PROMPTS

1. Supergirl has the same superpowers as the Man of Steel, including super-strength. Locate other panels in this book where Supergirl demonstrates her Kryptonian powers.

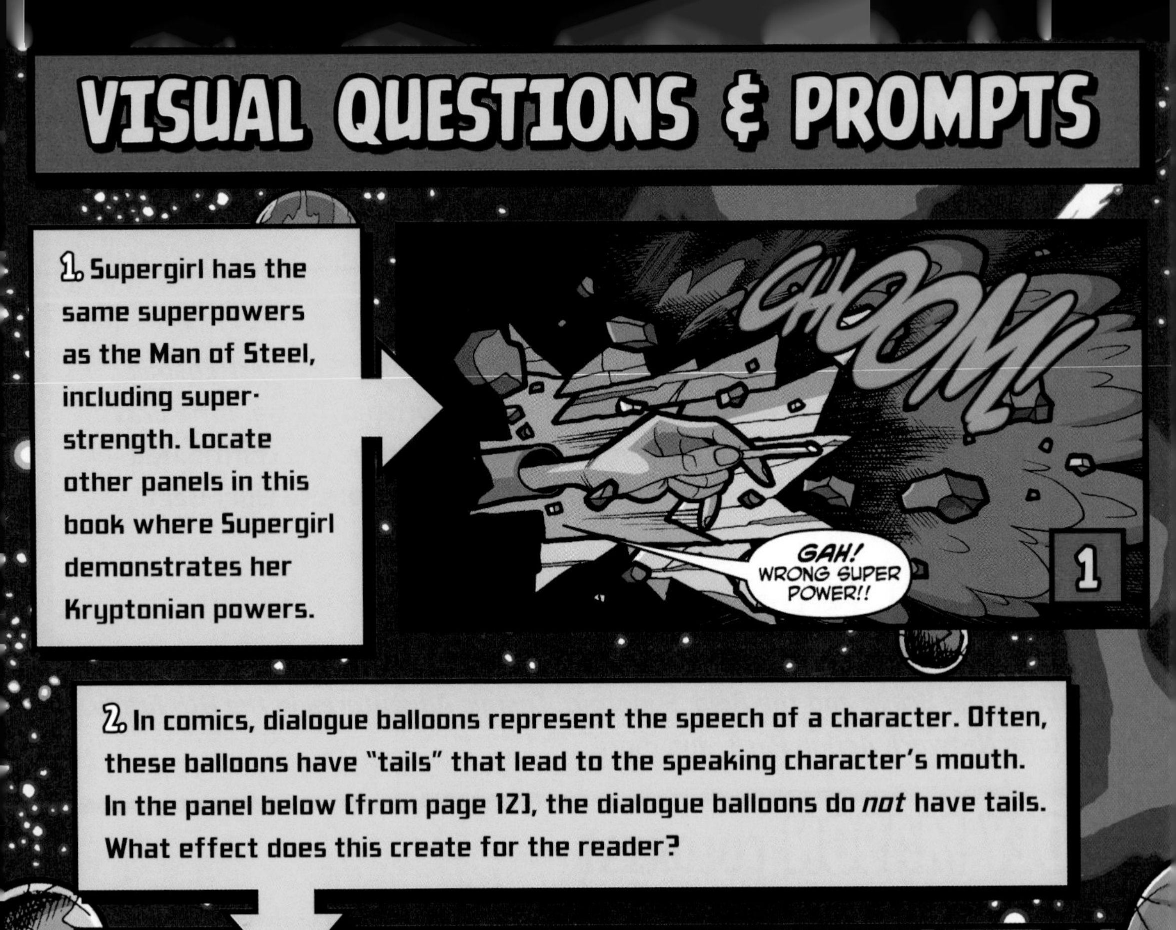
CHOOOM!
GAH! WRONG SUPER POWER!!
1

2. In comics, dialogue balloons represent the speech of a character. Often, these balloons have "tails" that lead to the speaking character's mouth. In the panel below (from page 12), the dialogue balloons do *not* have tails. What effect does this create for the reader?

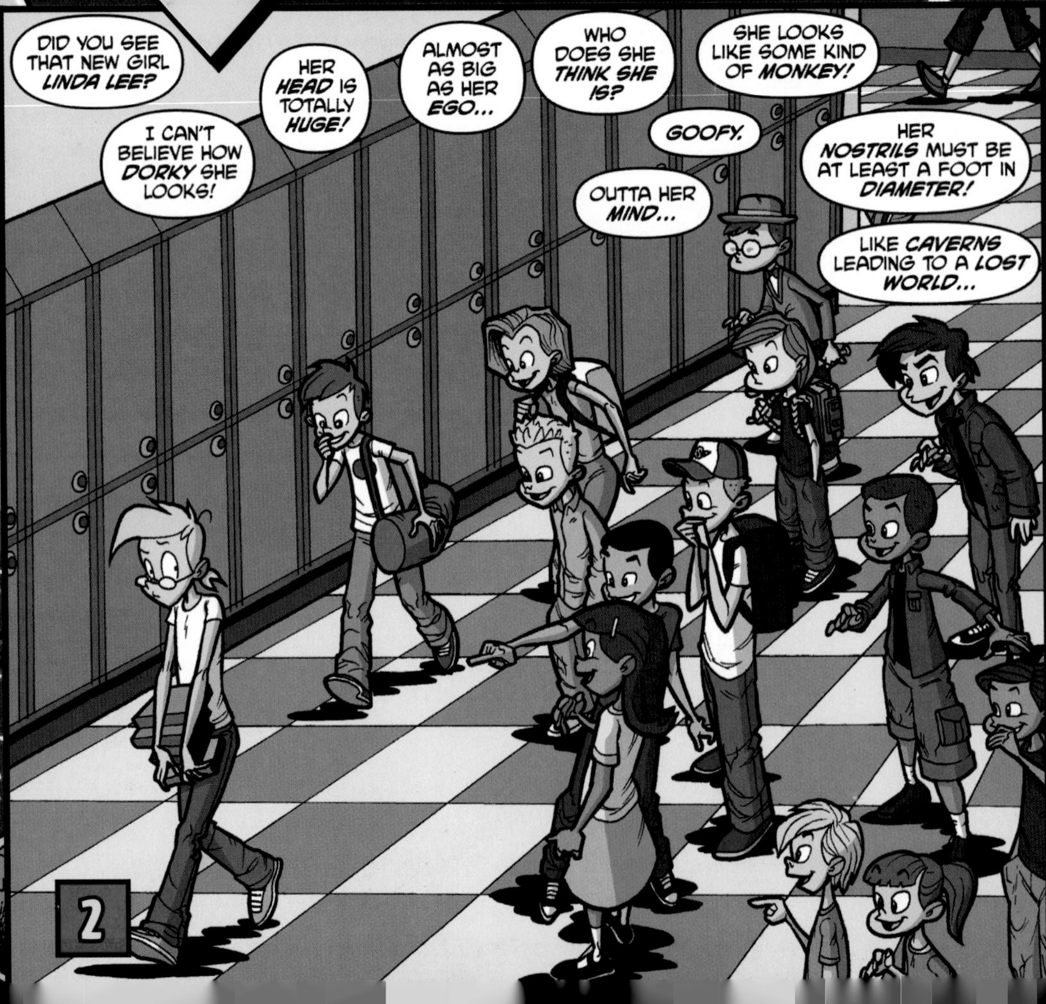
DID YOU SEE THAT NEW GIRL LINDA LEE?
I CAN'T BELIEVE HOW DORKY SHE LOOKS!
HER HEAD IS TOTALLY HUGE!
ALMOST AS BIG AS HER EGO...
WHO DOES SHE THINK SHE IS?
SHE LOOKS LIKE SOME KIND OF MONKEY!
GOOFY.
OUTTA HER MIND...
HER NOSTRILS MUST BE AT LEAST A FOOT IN DIAMETER!
LIKE CAVERNS LEADING TO A LOST WORLD...
2

3. The way a character's eyes and mouth are illustrated can tell a lot about the emotions he or she is feeling. How do you think Supergirl is feeling in the panel at right [from page 11]? Describe how you can tell.

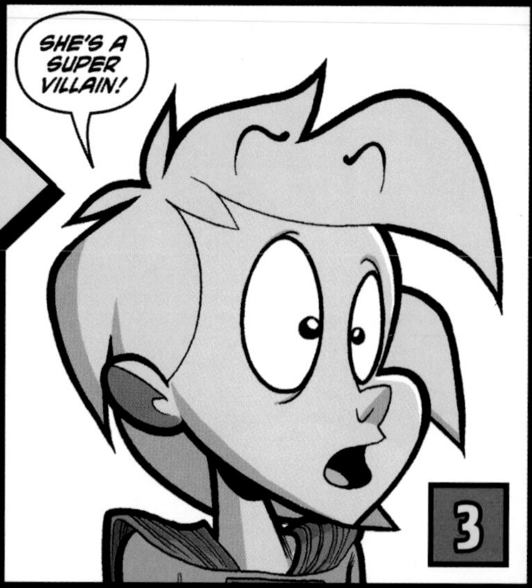

SHE'S A SUPER VILLAIN!
3

4. Comic illustrators often add visual clues about the story to come. In the panel below [from page 18], the illustrator magnified the recorder in Belinda's hand. Why do you think he chose to draw attention to this object?

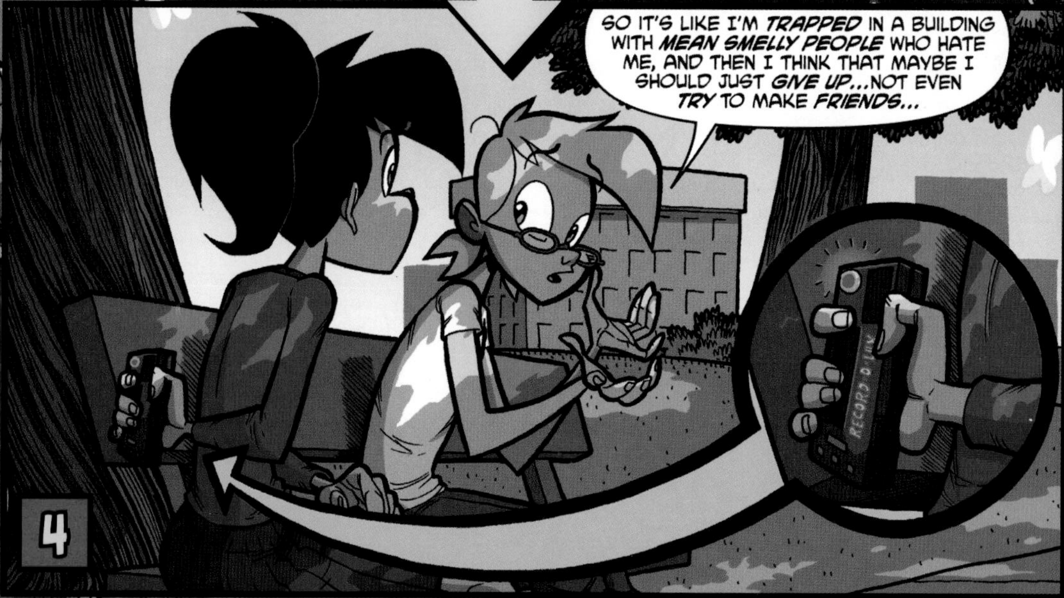

SO IT'S LIKE I'M TRAPPED IN A BUILDING WITH MEAN SMELLY PEOPLE WHO HATE ME, AND THEN I THINK THAT MAYBE I SHOULD JUST GIVE UP...NOT EVEN TRY TO MAKE FRIENDS...
RECORDING
4

5. What did you learn about Lena Thorul's character from this email [shown on page 26]? Do you think she is a good or evil character? Explain your answer.

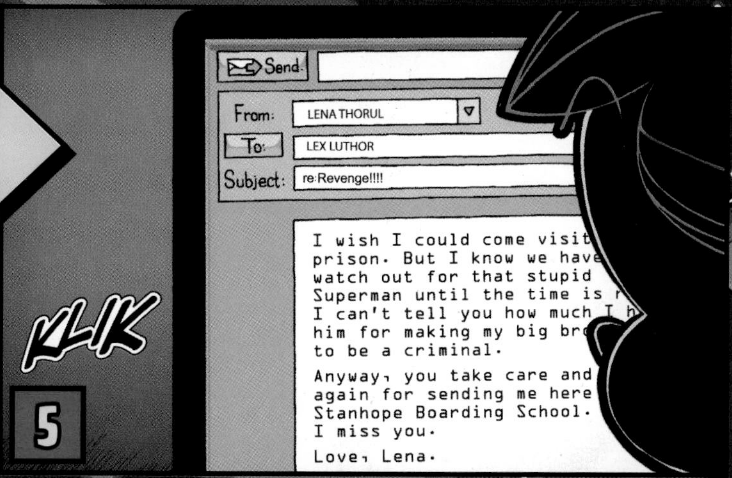

Send
From: LENA THORUL
To: LEX LUTHOR
Subject: re:Revenge!!!!
I wish I could come visit
prison. But I know we have
watch out for that stupid
Superman until the time is
I can't tell you how much I
him for making my big
to be a criminal.
Anyway, you take care and
again for sending me here
Stanhope Boarding School.
I miss you.
Love, Lena.
KLIK
5

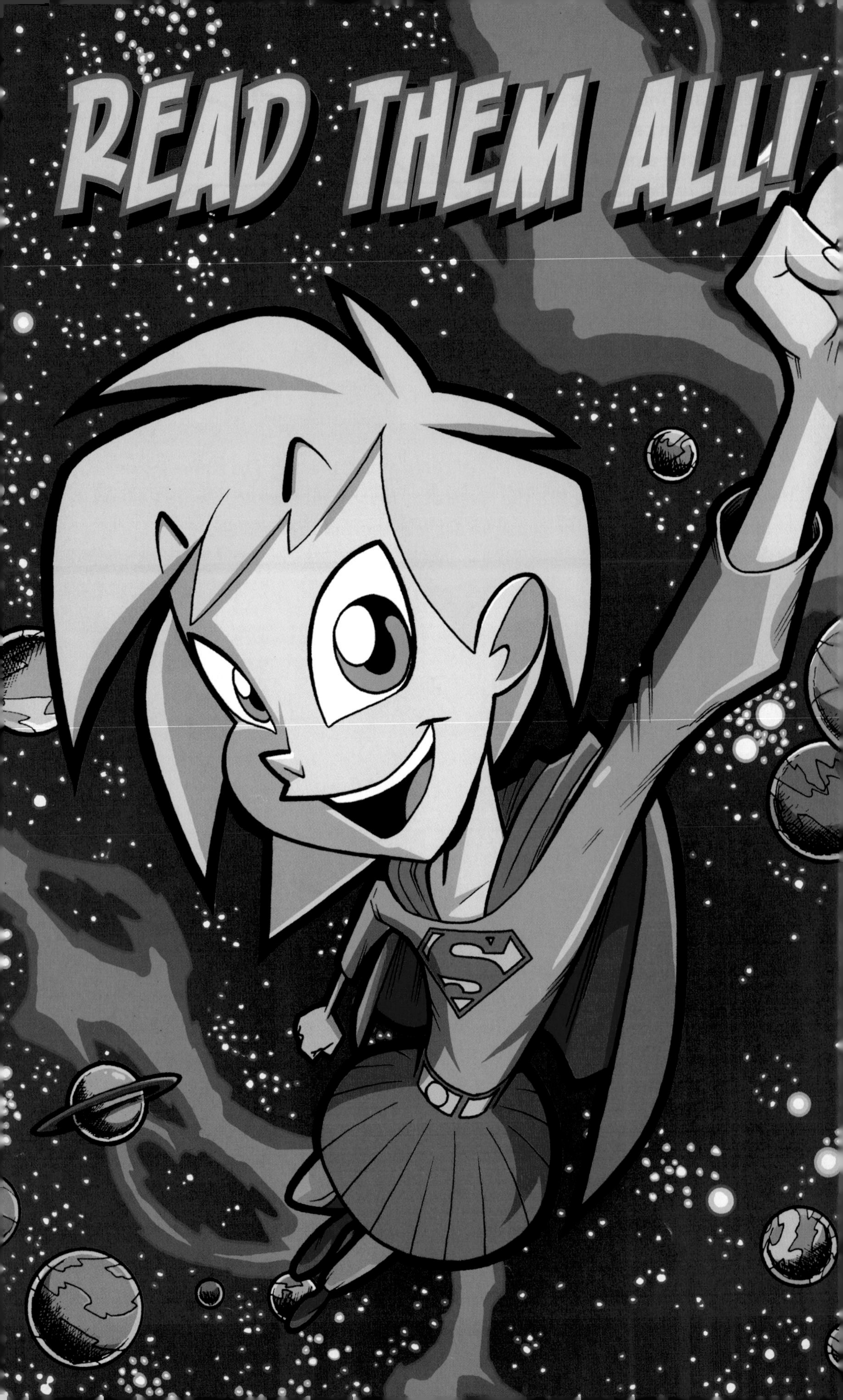
READ THEM ALL!

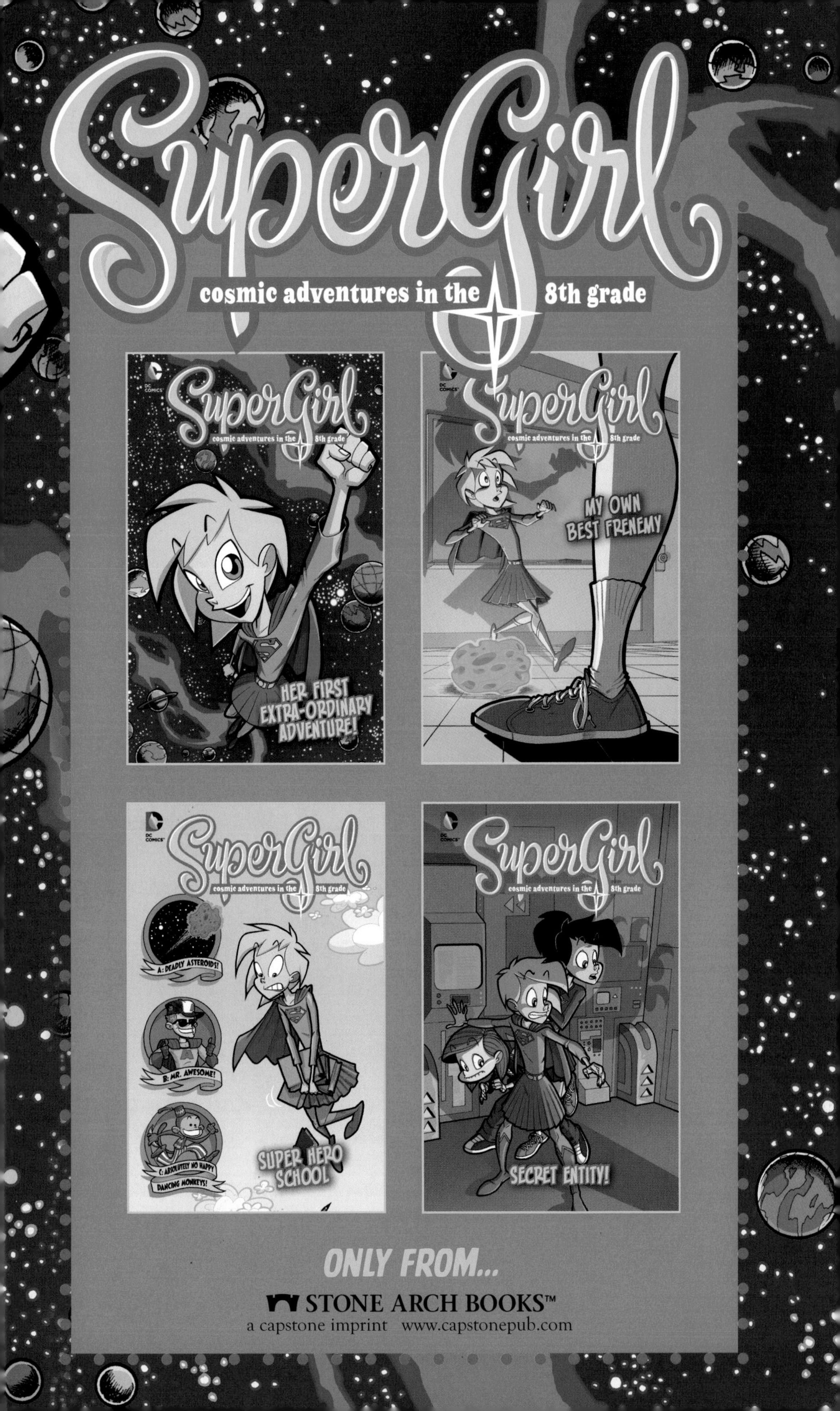
SuperGirl
cosmic adventures in the 8th grade
DC COMICS
SuperGirl
cosmic adventures in the 8th grade
HER FIRST EXTRA-ORDINARY ADVENTURE!
DC COMICS
SuperGirl
cosmic adventures in the 8th grade
MY OWN BEST FRENEMY
DC COMICS
SuperGirl
cosmic adventures in the 8th grade
A: DEADLY ASTEROIDS!
B: MR. AWESOME!
C: ABSOLUTELY NO HAPPY DANCING MONKEYS!
SUPER HERO SCHOOL
DC COMICS
SuperGirl
cosmic adventures in the 8th grade
SECRET ENTITY!
ONLY FROM...
STONE ARCH BOOKS™
a capstone imprint www.capstonepub.com

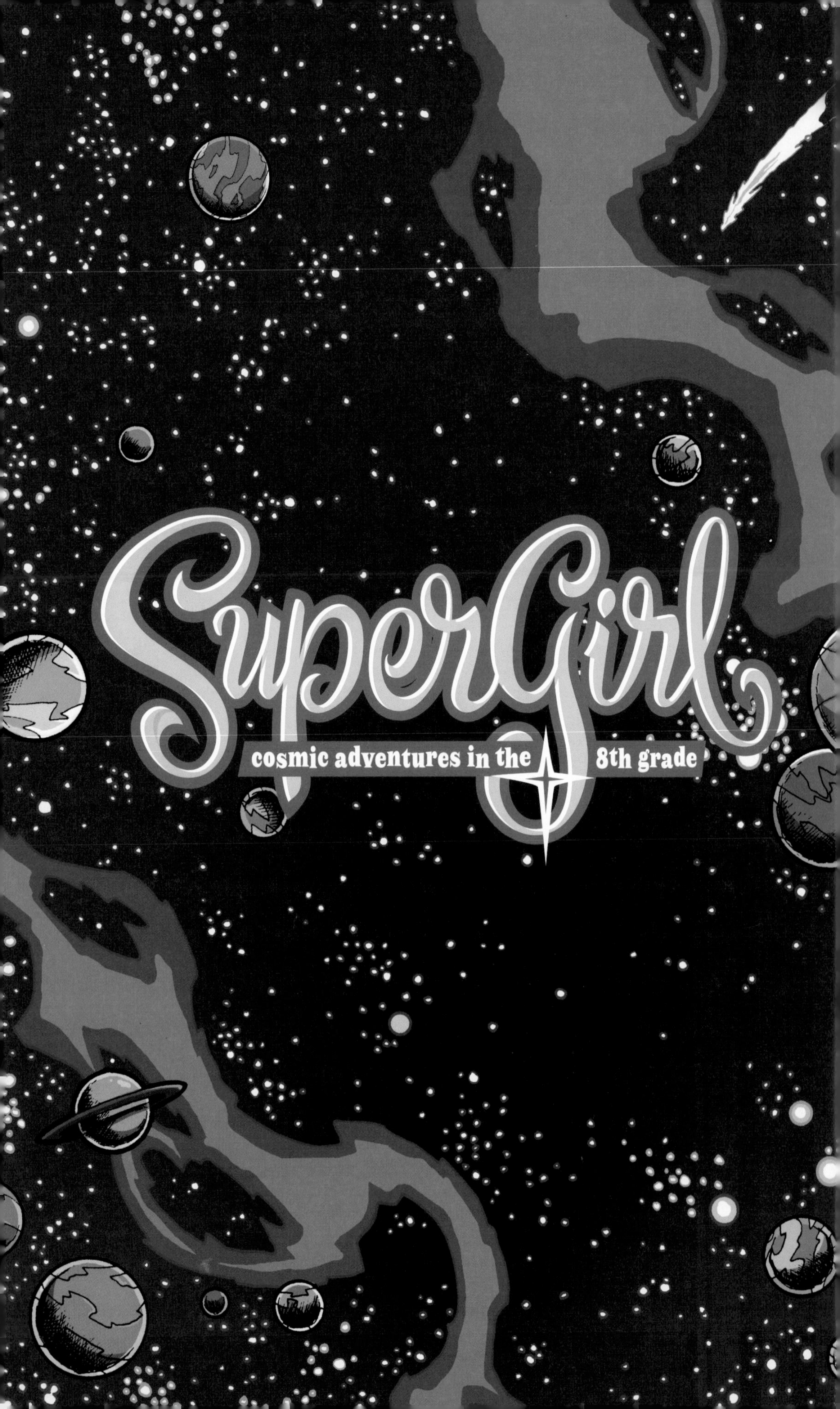
SuperGirl
cosmic adventures in the 8th grade